There's nowhere to run . . .

Jessica felt a wave of panic rise inside of her as James tightened his arms around her, pulling her to the ground.

"James!" she cried. "Stop it. Get off me!" Jessica beat on his back with her fists, screaming.

But James's only response was to cover her mouth with his and plant a wet, sloppy kiss on her lips. She jerked her head away and tried to sit up. "Get off me!" she shouted again.

Suddenly, James scrambled to his feet. He leaned down and grabbed her by the upper arm. "It's too cold out here," he said in a thick voice. "Let's get in the car."

Jessica half-lay on the ground, her feet dragging along the dirt. "Quit playing games, Jessica," James yelled. And with that, he lifted her up and carried her toward the car.

"No!" Jessica shrieked at the top of her lungs.

But there was no one to hear her. No one for miles around.

Bantam Books in the Sweet Valley University series
Ask your bookseller for the books you have missed

SWEET VALLEY UNIVERSITY™

No Means No

Written by
Laurie John

Created by
FRANCINE PASCAL

BANTAM BOOKS
NEW YORK · TORONTO · LONDON · SYDNEY · AUCKLAND

RL 6, age 12 and up

NO MEANS NO

A Bantam Book / March 1995

Sweet Valley High® and Sweet Valley University™
are trademarks of Francine Pascal
Conceived by Francine Pascal
Produced by Daniel Weiss Associates, Inc.
33 West 17th Street
New York, NY 10011

ISBN: 0-553-56655-5

Published simultaneously in the United States and Canada

Bantam Books are published by Bantam Books, a division of Bantam
Doubleday Dell Publishing Group, Inc. Its trademark, consisting of the
words "Bantam Books" and the portrayal of a rooster, is Registered in
U.S. Patent and Trademark Office and in other countries. Marca
Registrada. Bantam Books, 1540 Broadway, New York, New York 10036.

PRINTED IN THE UNITED STATES OF AMERICA

OPM   0 9 8 7 6 5 4 3 2 1

To Billy Carmen

Chapter One

Lila Fowler let out a long, liquid scream of pure terror.

Three yards away stood the most horrifying creature she had ever seen. A wolf. A silver wolf with eyes like transparent glass.

Her eyes were drawn to his gleaming white fangs. Everything else seemed blurred and unreal. The surrounding trees. The distant wreckage of the plane. The blue sky with its billowing clouds. None of it was real anymore.

The scene began to unfold in slow motion. Lila felt as if she and the wolf were suspended in oil. Hands, legs, and feet moved sluggishly, one or two seconds out of sync with real time.

The muscles in the wolf's shoulders and hips bunched as he gathered his legs beneath him to spring from his perch on the rocky ledge.

1

She had screamed moments ago, but the sound was only now beginning to reverberate through the woods. It seemed to echo back forever. There was a rustle and stir in the treetops, and suddenly a dark cloud of birds rose up and flew away, wings furiously beating against the sky.

I'm going to die, Lila thought.

She stood still as the wolf lunged. *Please let it be quick,* she thought in desperation. *I don't want to suffer*.

Fangs, claws, and ninety pounds of predatory muscle hurtled toward her and then . . . astonishingly . . . . veered away seconds before his jaws made contact with her flesh.

What's happening? What's going on? she wondered.

The wolf fell back a few steps and snarled, pacing nervously back and forth.

Then Lila understood. The wolf didn't know what kind of creature she was. He had no idea what to expect from her. Flight? Claws? Brute strength?

The wolf whined in confusion, then lifted his lips again in a snarl. "Come on. Come on," the wolf seemed to be saying. "Show me something. Show me what you are."

Lila was determined to show no fear. "I'm not taking any crap off some overgrown yard dog," she muttered. She took an experimental step forward, and the growling became more intense.

Lila watched the wolf's muscles tense in preparation for another lunge.

This time she was going to be ready. She slowly leaned down and closed her hand over a small, loose branch. The bark was rough and dotted with knotty lumps.

Lila felt the bumps dig into the soft flesh of her hands. Three manicures a week didn't do much to toughen the palms. But she felt no pain. Fear had made her numb.

The wolf began pacing again. He was hungry, but he was nervous. Lila took a step back. If she could get to what was left of the body of the wrecked plane, she could barricade herself in the cockpit.

Lila took another step back. The wolf sat down and whined, lifting his head and sniffing her scent on the air.

She took another step back, and he jumped to his feet and began to growl. Her heart sank as he slunk forward with a lowered head.

Fear made her breath come in short gasps. A surge of adrenaline coursed through her veins, sparking her nerve endings back to life and animating her emotions. She readied herself for the attack.

This time when the wolf sprang, he sprang for real, leaving the ground in two stages. First came the heavily muscled shoulders and the terrifying head. Then came the powerful flanks and hind paws.

Lila lifted her branch. *Please let me have enough strength,* she prayed. *Please.*

A savage cry tore through the still air as the wolf sailed toward her, his jaws aimed right at her throat.

Wait until you see the whites of his eyes, she warned herself. *Wait for the right moment. You can't afford to miss.* With every ounce of strength and courage she possessed, Lila forced herself to wait . . . wait . . . wait . . .

The wolf was so close she could feel his hot breath.

NOW!

She swung with all her might. The branch connected with the wolf's skull and snapped into two pieces. The impact was so forceful that Lila shrieked as red hot pain traveled up her arm and set fire to her shoulder.

The wolf let out a surprised yip and fell to the ground. He lay there for a moment, stunned.

Lila's legs began to shake, and the piercing ache in her arm was causing big black dots to form in front of her eyes. She dropped the stick and ran almost blindly back toward the cockpit. There

4

wasn't much time. The wolf was going to be on his feet in a matter of seconds.

Behind her she heard a growl and whine. After that the sound of padded feet loping across the bed of crackling leaves that covered the ground.

"Help!" she screamed, even though there was no one to hear. "Help!"

The half-destroyed cockpit of the wrecked plane beckoned like an oasis. But the harder she ran, the farther away it seemed to be.

Lila lowered her head and poured every remaining ounce of strength into her legs. Behind her she sensed the animal springing. *At least I tried,* she thought as she pitched forward. *At least I didn't go down without a fight.*

Where's Bruce? she wondered wildly. Would he be sorry he had baited her into going up with him in his new plane? Would he be sorry that he'd stalked off in a fit of anger and left her all alone?

Would he be sorry she was dead?

"So anyway," Jessica Wakefield chattered happily, "I went to Professor Martin's office dressed as Liz and I carried a tape recorder in my pocket."

James's lips traveled the line of Jessica's jaw, and a thousand butterflies took flight in her stomach. That made it very hard to converse. "James, are you listening to me?"

"Sort of," James murmured, pressing his face into her neck. Jessica unwound his arms from around her waist and studied his handsome face. His clean-cut good looks were a refreshing change from the dark, slightly unkempt appeal of Michael McAllery, the man she had impulsively married for a few disastrous weeks.

James seemed to be studying her face, too, and he looked pleased with what he saw. Jessica tossed her long blond hair off her shoulder and widened her blue-green eyes for maximum effect. The results were very satisfactory. His face broke into a melting smile, and he leaned forward to kiss her again.

"I'm trying to talk to you," she said, rearing back in mock indignation. "How can I talk to you if you're going to make it impossible for me to think about unpleasant subjects?"

James wrapped his arms loosely around her waist. "If a subject is unpleasant, then let's not think about it." He leaned back against the concrete wall of the athletic facility and locker rooms that were attached to the Sweet Valley University stadium. Gently he pulled her toward him and kissed her cheek.

"James," she said.

His lips moved to hers.

"James!" she said again. All this admiration and affection was nice, but it could wait. She was bursting to finish her story before he had to leave. The game wouldn't start for another hour, but the coach wanted the players present and suited up at least a half hour before the game started.

He planted a kiss on the tip of her nose.

Jessica pulled away. "James! The subject may be unpleasant. But it's about me and it's important. And if you would listen to me for five minutes, you'd find out there's an extremely happy ending."

James's face was immediately contrite. "I'm sorry, Jess. If it's important to you, it's important to me."

"Yo, James! How's it going?"

Two of James's teammates came hurrying by on their way to the locker room. Seconds later three more guys came around the stadium, and James gave them a genial wave. Then he turned his attention back to Jessica. "You were saying?"

"I went to Professor Martin's office," Jessica began again, "and . . ."

But before she could finish her sentence, a tall, good-looking senior appeared and clapped a huge hand down on one of James's shoulders. Jessica recognized him as Mo Bentley, the student assistant coach. "Mind suiting up a little early? I'd like to go over some plays with you."

James nodded. "Sure. I'll be right there."

"See you in the locker room." Mo winked at Jessica before he left.

"Now," James said again. "You went to Professor Martin's office with a tape recorder and . . ."

Jessica rolled her eyes and smiled reluctantly. "This is impossible. I can't tell you a complicated story if fifty million people are going to interrupt us."

"Can I help it if I'm a big football hero?" he asked with a laugh.

Jessica giggled and shook her head. "No. And I love that you're a big football hero. Don't stop being one on my account."

He looked around with comic furtiveness and pulled Jessica around the corner of the building. "Okay," he whispered. "We're alone. You've got my undivided attention. Now shoot."

As Jessica began to tell him how Alison Quinn, the stuck-up vice president of the Theta Alpha Theta sorority, had set her up, her eyes grew clouded.

Even though Jessica had never actually joined the prestigious sorority, she had been a star pledge. But on the day of initiation, she hadn't shown up for the ceremony. Mike McAllery hadn't wanted her to.

After that she had been in semi-disgrace with most of the Thetas. Once her brief and unhappy marriage with Mike was behind her, though, she had been eager to become a pledge again.

But Alison Quinn despised Jessica. She'd said that if Jessica wanted to repledge, she was going to have to prove her loyalty to the sorority. So she'd issued Jessica a dare: to sneak into Professor Martin's office and steal one of his prized first editions.

Jessica accepted the challenge, and that night, dressed all in black, she'd sneaked into Professor Martin's office. But the second she removed the book from the shelf, the lights had come on with a blaze and a deep voice had told her to freeze. Two uniformed guards from campus security caught her red-handed.

Instead of standing behind Jessica, Alison had claimed she knew nothing about the prank and tried to have Jessica permanently barred from the sorority because of her "criminal background."

"Elizabeth and I both wondered two things," Jessica said, enjoying the firm and supportive squeeze James gave her upper arm. "First of all, how did security know I was going to be there?

9

And how were we going to get Professor Martin to drop the charges?"

James smiled. "Aha. I wondered when Elizabeth was going to make an appearance in this story."

Jessica began to laugh. "You know, James, it's unbelievable how handy it is to have an identical twin. I don't know how people get through life who don't have one."

Jessica and Elizabeth Wakefield had caused a lot of confusion on the Sweet Valley University campus when they arrived. They were mirror images of each other—on the outside. Their long golden blond hair and sparkling aquamarine eyes were identical. They even had the same dimple in their left cheeks when they smiled.

But when it came to personalities and interests, they were as different as night and day. Jessica was flirtatious, impulsive, and never happy being out of the spotlight for long. She considered it her duty to keep Elizabeth's life exciting. And Jessica didn't hesitate to pretend to be her twin when she got in a jam—much to Elizabeth's consternation.

Elizabeth was straightforward, serious about school, and content to accomplish her goals behind the scenes. Whenever Jessica created trouble—which was often—Elizabeth ended up rushing around, trying to undo the damage and smooth things over. Without fail, Elizabeth would save her twin from imminent disaster.

Jessica couldn't help smiling as she remembered the brilliance of her latest performance as Elizabeth. "You may already know this," she said, "but Professor Martin has a pretty bad reputation for leching on the freshman girls."

"I've heard things," James replied. "But I don't know anything for sure."

Jessica smiled. "Well, actually, I didn't *know* either, but Elizabeth *suspected*. Every time she was in his office, he sat really close and was always finding some excuse to touch her." Jessica gave a little involuntary shiver of revulsion.

James lifted an eyebrow but said nothing.

"So I dressed up like Elizabeth, went to his office with a tape recorder, and then just waited for him to do his stuff. When he made a move on me, I got it all on tape. Than I agreed not to press sexual harassment charges if he agreed to drop the charges against me—*and* keep his hands off Elizabeth."

James threw back his head and laughed. "Poor guy."

Jessica blinked. "Poor guy? What do you mean, *poor guy*? He's a creep."

"He may be a creep. But guys have been coming

11

on to girls since the dawn of time, and now suddenly it's illegal." James shrugged. "Is that fair?"

Jessica's heart gave an uncomfortable flutter. Maybe she hadn't told the story right. Or maybe James hadn't been paying attention. Professor Martin wasn't just some guy coming on to a girl. He was a first-class jerk. She took a hesitant step away from James.

"What's the matter?" James reached for her hand.

Jessica shook her head. "There's something really wrong to me about feeling sorry for Professor Martin. Something weird about acting like what Elizabeth and I did wasn't fair. I don't think Professor Martin can act the way he does and then complain that somebody didn't treat him *fairly*."

James held on to her arms with two hands now and stared into her eyes. "Hey!" he said quickly. "Don't get upset. I'm on your side, Jess. I'm always on your side."

She felt her body relax. James was right. Why was she getting so bent out of shape? Professor Martin and his wandering hands were history. The lowlife had dropped the charges and hopefully learned a good lesson.

Jessica stared at James's handsome face. His

bright blue eyes stood out against the rugged planes of his tanned face. His square jaw looked like it was cut from stone. He probably just had a really hard time understanding things from a girl's point of view.

"Jessica," he said in a comforting voice, "the only person I care about getting treated fairly is you. What you want, I want. So what about the Thetas? Will they take you back as a pledge now that the charges have been dropped?"

"I think so," she said with a sly smile. "Elizabeth did a little private investigative work. She got the guy over at the campus security office to show her the phone log from the past few days. Turns out they only had one phone call the night of the break-in." Jessica paused.

"So?"

"It was placed from Theta House."

James's eyes opened wide. "Theta House? Are you saying somebody called from Theta House and tipped off security?"

Jessica nodded, and her face darkened. "No doubt about it. Alison Quinn set me up."

James whistled. "Wow. What are you going to do?"

"I'm going to tell the Thetas what I know. And then I'm going to let them make up their own minds."

James was silent for a few moments. "Be careful," he said finally. "Take it from the meanest guy on the field—I'd rather face a line of Green Bay Packers than go up against Alison Quinn. She's not going to give up."

Jessica shook her head. She refused to be daunted. Things were going too well for her now. The gods of college were on her side. "Me neither," she said lightly.

"I'm serious," James said. "Alison doesn't mind fighting dirty if she has to."

"Neither do I," Jessica repeated.

James lifted an eyebrow. "That makes three of us." With a growl, he pulled Jessica off balance so that she fell against his chest and into a tight embrace. "Gotcha!"

Jessica laughed happily as James smothered her face with kisses.

"Hey, James!"

James reluctantly released Jessica, and she pushed her tousled blond hair off her forehead. Mo Bentley stood several yards away in classic jock stance. Feet apart. Hands on hips. "You planning to play today, Romeo?" he called.

James held up his hands. "I'm coming, I'm coming."

Mo grinned at Jessica. "I just want to borrow him. You can have him back after the game."

"Thanks," Jessica joked. "But return him in good shape. No dents or scratches, please."

The guys laughed appreciatively, and Mo disappeared around the corner.

James squeezed Jessica's hand in an affectionate good-bye. "So when do I get to formally meet the amazing Elizabeth?" James asked. "I saw her at the high school reunion, but we never actually talked."

"You'll meet her this afternoon," Jessica promised. "After the game, at the tailgate picnic."

James nodded. "Sounds good. Think she'll approve of me?"

"Can you think of any reason why she shouldn't?" Jessica teased.

James rubbed a rueful hand over his chin. "I'm afraid not. We premed types are pretty boring."

"Well, there's nothing boring about you on the football field." She laughed. Then she gave him a gentle push toward the locker room. "Get going before Mo comes back and yells at me."

James grinned. "Sit close to the field so I can see you. Okay?"

"I will," Jessica promised as she backed away, reluctantly letting her fingers slip away from his.

"Why are you being so prickly?" Elizabeth Wakefield asked.

15

"Who's prickly?" Maia Stillwater demanded.

"You are," Elizabeth said. "That's about the third time this morning that you've snapped at me."

"Sorry," Maia said abruptly. She turned her gaze back down to her notebook.

The two girls were sitting in the dorm room in Dickenson Hall that Elizabeth and Jessica shared. They were working on a journalism assignment. "Collaborate on a fifteen-hundred-word editorial on any gender issue that is topical. Make sure you express a definite point of view," the professor had instructed.

Elizabeth and Maia had been spitballing ideas for the last half hour, trying to come up with a topic and point of view. Elizabeth had made several suggestions, but Maia had shot most of them down.

Elizabeth bit her lower lip, not quite knowing what to make of Maia's behavior. Elizabeth had always heard great things about Maia, but until recently she'd barely known her. It was only since they wound up in the same journalism class this semester that they'd become friends. And Elizabeth had thought everything she'd been told about Maia being smart, funny, and sensitive was true—until they'd tried to work together.

At first Elizabeth had been delighted to be

partnered with Maia. Now she felt like she was working with someone she didn't even know, and at the rate they were going, they would never get this assignment done.

"What about an editorial calling for an SVU consensual sex policy?" she suggested. "I just read a magazine article about two college campuses that recently instituted them. It really got students to think and talk about the issue of date rape."

Maia dutifully added Elizabeth's idea to the list of possible topics, but as she did, she sighed and rolled her eyes.

It took every ounce of Elizabeth's self-control to keep the impatience she felt out of her voice. "It's a timely subject, and I think it would make a good paper."

"Whatever you say," Maia muttered.

That did it. "All right, forget what I say!" Elizabeth cried in frustration. "What do *you* say?"

"If you want to know the truth, I think writing about this stuff is a waste of time."

"Look, Maia," Elizabeth said slowly, "you may not think that rape and sexual abuse on college campuses is a big problem, but I've been reading some of the studies, and I can tell you—"

"You can't tell me anything I don't already

know," Maia snapped. "But if you think a consensual sex policy is the answer, you're nuts."

Elizabeth took two deep breaths and then began to speak. "I'm not saying it's *the* answer. I'm saying it might be a decent first step. If you institute a consensual sex policy, then guys at least have to ask. And they can't say later that it was all just a *misunderstanding*."

Maia closed her notebook with a snap. "Elizabeth, sometimes you are very naive. Any guy who's willing to play *Mother May I* is probably not the guy you need to be afraid of." Maia jumped to her feet and began angrily gathering her books and papers.

Elizabeth gaped at Maia. She had never seen her so angry. Collaboration was always difficult, but this was out of control. "Maia," she said in a soothing voice, "calm down." She reached up and took Maia's hand. "I know we're working on a short deadline and this is an important paper, but it's not the end of the world. It's just a journalism assignment, okay?"

Maia stared at Elizabeth. Her breathing began to slow, and the color in her cheeks began to fade. Her eyes were still troubled, but she gave Elizabeth a reluctant, embarrassed smile. "I guess the pressure is getting to me. I'm sorry."

Elizabeth stood and poured some soda into a

paper cup. "Have something to drink. It's hot in here."

Maia gratefully took the cup and sat down on Elizabeth's bed. "I've pulled two all-nighters in a row," she admitted, lowering her eyes. "I think I'm crashing."

Elizabeth felt an enormous rush of relief. If Maia had been up for two days straight, that would explain why she was feeling so irritable. It didn't have anything to do with Elizabeth or their collaboration.

Elizabeth closed her own notebook and put it on her desk. "Let's table this for a while. We've still got a few days, and we can take another crack at it when you're rested." She walked over and threw open the window. "Let's get some fresh air in here," she said.

Maia smiled thinly and bent her head to take another sip of soda.

Elizabeth leaned out the window and took a few deep breaths. "Perfect football weather," she commented happily. She turned slightly to check her reflection in the dresser mirror and couldn't help being satisfied by what she saw. The first few weeks of school had been such an unhappy time that Elizabeth had turned to salt, grease, and sugar for comfort. It hadn't taken long for her to put on fifteen pounds.

But Elizabeth had fought back. The weight was off now, and she was back to her old self.

The tall blond with the blue-green eyes who smiled back from the mirror was a perfect size six in snug jeans, a forest-green cotton turtleneck, and an oversized cardigan with big silver buttons.

Something about the air, the excitement of the big game, and the pure joy of being young with everything ahead of her produced a rush of euphoria. Finally she was part of the college scene she had always dreamed of. Challenging classes. Intellectual debate. And lots and lots of sunny afternoons with Tom Watts. She glanced at her watch and felt a little flutter of anticipation around her shoulder blades. Tom should be arriving any minute.

Beneath the window she could see groups of students streaming in the direction of the stadium. "Wow! It looks like the whole campus is turning out for the football game."

Maia came over to the window and stood beside her. "You'd think people in college would find something more productive to do than waste their time sitting around watching a bunch of Neanderthals fool around with a ball," she commented sourly.

Elizabeth felt her mood sink a little. Was Maia going to be negative about every single thing in the world?

There was a knock at the door, and Elizabeth felt her heart skip a beat. She hurried to greet Tom, ready to get out of this hot, stuffy room and away from Maia's grumpiness.

"Hi, there," Tom said, dropping a kiss on her blond head. "Hi, Maia!"

Maia didn't turn from the window. "Hi," she mumbled, keeping her back to him.

Tom raised his eyebrows and threw an interrogative look at Elizabeth.

Elizabeth shrugged. What could she say? Maia was in a crummy mood, and that's all there was to it. Still, she felt a flicker of irritation as she glanced at Maia's rigid back. Tom looked like a movie star and came off as the most secure guy in the whole world. But Elizabeth knew that he was extremely sensitive and self-critical. Like her, he was probably wondering what in the world he'd done to offend Maia.

Elizabeth walked past him and brushed her lips over his ear. "She's in a bad mood," she whispered softly. "Don't take it personally."

Tom gave a little nod to signal that he understood. "I made some sandwiches," Elizabeth said brightly. She reached for the small basket she had packed with sandwiches, bottles of mineral water, and some crisp red apples she'd bought from a farmers' market.

"Great," Tom said. He jerked his head toward Maia and seemed to ask a question.

Elizabeth shrugged. What was he getting at?

He raised his eyebrows.

Again Elizabeth shrugged.

Tom threw up his hands and took a deep breath. "Maia, why don't you come to the game with us? I'll split my sandwich with you. And if it's salami, you can even have it all. Now, is that a deal or what?"

Elizabeth couldn't help smiling. She was so lucky to have Tom. Most guys would never have invited a third wheel along on a date. Particularly a wheel that wasn't even friendly that day.

"No, thanks," Maia said shortly.

"It's one of the biggest games of the season," Elizabeth coaxed. "Where's your team spirit?"

"I said no," Maia repeated evenly, turning from the window and fixing Tom with a level, almost hostile stare. "I don't have any team spirit. And I don't like jocks."

Tom visibly flinched, and Elizabeth gasped. "Maia!"

Even though Tom had quit the football team after his freshman year, he still had the size and build of a superb athlete. And the "legend of Tom Watts" lived on, despite his attempts to downplay his jock image.

Maia immediately colored and dropped her eyes. "I'm sorry," she said. "I didn't mean you. Really," she added. She quickly bent and scooped up her backpack and notebook. "I need to get some sleep. I'll see you guys later."

"Wow!" Tom said as soon as she was out the door. "Remind me not to get on her bad side."

"You're telling me," Elizabeth said. She grabbed her keys off the desk and stuffed them down in her pocket. Tom picked up the picnic basket, and the two of them left the dorm room.

"She said she's been up for two nights straight," Elizabeth said.

Tom laughed. "That'll do strange things to your personality."

Elizabeth tried to smile, but somehow Maia's bitterness had taken a little of her pleasure out of the sunny day.

She felt Tom's hand tighten over hers and tug. "Hey," he said softly. "You look a little pale yourself. If you'd rather skip the game, that's okay with me. I don't have a whole lot of team spirit myself. But I do like sitting next to pretty blondes on a cool day and eating sandwiches."

"And this blonde wants to go to the game. Actually, I have to go. Jessica's finally going to officially introduce me to James Montgomery. He's a star player on the team, you know."

"Ohhhhh. Now I see why you wanted to go to the game today. I should have known there was a hidden motive."

"Sure." She laughed. "People always act like Jessica's got the patent on hidden motives, but I've usually got one or two up my sleeve."

Chapter Two

The wolf lunged at the fiberglass body of the cockpit, half-crazed with hunger and frustration. Saliva foamed around his mouth, and Lila thought she had never heard such hideous noises from any creature in her whole life.

She still couldn't believe she had made it this far. His snapping jaws had missed her by inches when she leapt from the ground, pulled herself up on the wing, and then made her way down the slant of the fuselage to the nose of the plane, which rested on the ground.

One side of the cockpit was partially caved in from landing, but the other side was mostly intact. The windshield was gone and so was some of the door, but at least there was only one way in to get her. As long as she could defend that opening, she was safe.

"Get away!" she shrieked.

But her voice just enraged the wolf further, and he lunged again. The force of his body hit the lightweight fuselage and a panel of it fell away, leaving her more exposed.

She leaned out and snatched up the panel, using it like a shield. When the wolf lunged again, she lifted the plate and heard his sharp claws slide along the metal surface.

With each lunge the impact sent shock waves up her already sore arm. She was in pain from her wrist to her shoulder socket. *I can't keep this up much longer.*

Another panel fell away from the cockpit. Sobbing with fatigue and terror, she instinctively scrooched farther back.

He lunged again.

This time the pain was so intense, her hand went numb and the strength left her fingers. The metal plate fell to the ground with a clang.

The wolf stood still a moment, then leapt toward her.

Lila kicked out with her leg, and his teeth closed with a snap over the leg of her thick sweatpants, ripping them open from thigh to ankle. He fell back with the piece of fabric in his mouth, growling and shaking it like a playful dog.

After a few moments the wolf dropped the cloth and turned his attention back to Lila. She closed her eyes, waiting. She couldn't fight back. Not anymore. This was it. Her life was over. What a horrible way to die.

There was a gruesome snarl and then . . .

"Hey, you! Hey, you! Look over here!"

Lila's eyes jerked open just in time to see Bruce hurl a rock toward the wolf. The rock glanced off his ear, and the wolf let out a yip of surprise.

Bruce waved his arms and jumped up and down. "Come on. Pick on somebody your own size!"

If Lila hadn't been so tired, terrified, and in pain, she would have laughed. The wolf whined in confusion, turning from Lila to Bruce, as if torn between the two targets.

"Come here, Fido!" Bruce yelled. He picked up another small stone and threw it.

The wolf began to run toward Bruce, picking up speed as he closed the distance between the cockpit of the plane and the perimeter of the clearing where Bruce stood.

Bruce glanced around, looking for a route of escape. But there wasn't one. The only retreat was into the woods, where the wolf would have the advantage.

It took Lila a split second to reach under the

copilot seat and locate the flare gun. She'd never fired one in her life, but some sixth sense guided her movements.

The wolf turned in mid-leap and let out a howl of fear as the hot red streak sizzled past his ears, leaving a trail of smoke. With his tail tucked between his legs, the wolf ran yipping into the forest.

Bruce didn't move. He stood there like a statue, looking completely stunned. After a few moments he slowly sank to his knees.

Lila jumped from what was left of the cockpit. "Bruce!" She ran toward him on legs that wobbled like a new foal's and collapsed next to him.

His eyes lifted and met hers. His tongue darted nervously over his lips. "We're alive," he said in a hoarse whisper. "Thanks to you."

Lila stared at Bruce. She'd known him practically all her life. For years, she had taken his good looks for granted. But now, with the shadow of stubble and the long scratch along his chin, it struck her that he was the handsomest man she had ever seen. "You saved me, Bruce," she said in a voice of dawning wonder. "You risked your own life to save mine."

"I kept picturing you the way you looked in first grade. All I knew was that I couldn't let you die," he said. "I couldn't imagine life without—" He broke off with a sob.

But he didn't have to finish. Lila knew what he meant. And she felt the same way.

"Ughhhhhhh!" Alexandra Rollins tipped carefully onto her side before opening her eyes. She had to move slowly so her brain didn't feel like it was floating around inside her head and bumping into the wall of her skull.

"Why do I do this to myself?" she mumbled.

She squeezed her eyes shut, wishing she were still asleep. Waking up was the worst. The absolute worst.

The first thing she always felt was that horrible hammering in the front of her head. The hammering that turned into a dull throb and didn't go away until she had her first drink of the day.

Her skull needed ventilation, but she knew the minute she opened her mouth and let in some fresh air, she'd taste her own morning breath. Her teeth would feel gummy. Her tongue would feel like cotton. Then her stomach would lurch, and she would be lucky if she made it to the bathroom before she puked. Two times out of three she had to settle for the wastebasket.

Alex opened her mouth and inhaled. Gag! Her mouth tasted like she had been sucking on wet cigars all night. When her stomach began to churn, she opened her mouth wider and took a couple of deep breaths. Sometimes that kept the nausea under control long enough for her to sit up and . . .

"Oh, jeez!" she moaned, sitting up and looking at the clock. It was late afternoon already. The day was gone. What happened?

Alex took a few more gulping breaths and dropped her head into her hands. Now came the worst part—remembering the night before.

Where had she been? Who had she been with? And what had she done?

Think, Alex, think. You must remember something. It's not really possible to lose great big chunks out of your life. Is it?

It is if you drink enough vodka, a little voice inside her head answered.

The more Alex strained to remember the night before, the worse her head hurt. And the worse her head hurt, the more nauseous she felt.

"I'll never drink again," Alex moaned as she reached for the wastebasket.

A few humiliating moments later Alex struggled into her robe and grabbed her shower things. When she got to the bathroom, she studiously avoided her reflection in the mirror while she brushed her teeth.

Judging from the magnitude of this hangover—which had to rate at least a ten on the

Richter scale—she wasn't a pretty sight.

She slipped off her robe and stepped into the shower, turning on both the hot and cold faucets full blast. She let the hard stream of the water pummel her shoulders while she racked her brains.

She smiled grimly at the slight memory of talking to Todd Wilkins last night. She had known him for years, and he had been Elizabeth's boyfriend all through high school.

In spite of the athletic-recruiting scandal that had sidelined Todd for the season and driven her own boyfriend, Mark Gathers, out of school, she still saw him as a slightly glamorous person. Somehow she felt like being seen with him might boost her own sagging prestige.

Both of them had been so miserable over the last few weeks that they had turned to each other for comfort. But she wasn't really sure what Todd was to her. Or what she was to Todd.

A date?

A friend?

A drinking buddy?

The answer was a little bit of all three. Which added up to a big nothing. And if she wanted to get brutally honest with herself, Todd had made that pretty clear recently.

So why couldn't she just stop thinking about him? Why, in spite of all the evidence to the contrary, did she keep seeing him as a big man on campus? And why, when she knew he didn't care beans about her, did she think being involved with him was going to solve any of her problems?

She quickly diverted her mind from that train of thought. Mark Gathers had given her enough rejection, heartache, and low self-esteem; she didn't need to mine her relationship with Todd for more.

A picture of Noah Pearson appeared in her mind. He was in her psychology class and always made a point of saying hello and giving her a friendly smile. The kind of friendly smile that made people feel good about themselves.

Why couldn't she attract somebody like that? Somebody kind and intelligent. He was good looking, too. Alex loved the way his shaggy, dark-blond hair and deep-set brown eyes suited the strong bones of his face.

He'd never be interested in somebody like me, she thought miserably, massaging some shampoo into her hair and rubbing her aching forehead.

There was a little worried tickling feeling in her stomach. She'd been supposed to do something today. What was it?

Oh, yeah. Her heart sank a little more. Today was the day of the big game. She should have been there, sitting with the rest of the Thetas.

By now the game must be over. She'd missed it, Alex realized with a sigh. Lately she'd missed more events than she had attended. There was a dinner tonight at Theta House. She should probably try to make it to that. There was a costume party at the Zeta house tonight, too. But she didn't think she could handle it. She felt too hung over. And too unhappy.

How did this happen? she wondered as she stepped out of the shower and wrapped her wet hair in a towel. *A few months ago my life was perfect. I'd gone from plain old Enid Rollins, the little brown hen, to Alexandra Rollins, a swan with a superjock boyfriend and a member of the most prestigious sorority on campus.*

Now her life was in the Dumpster. Being Enid, the little brown hen, would be a step up from Alexandra Rollins, has-been campus socialite.

She heard a group of girls chattering among themselves as they hurried down the hall outside the bathroom. They looked briefly through the open door. Seconds later Alex heard a burst of laughter as they descended the stairs to the lobby.

Her fingers gripped the edge of the sink. Were they laughing at her? Had she done something terrible and made a fool of herself last night? Was she now the official campus drunk?

Hot tears rolled down her cheeks as she stuffed her brush and makeup into her shower bag. She'd finish up in her room, where she wouldn't have to worry about someone walking in on her.

On the way out of the bathroom a flyer tacked to the bulletin board caught her eye.

FEELING ALL ALONE?
CALL THE CAMPUS HOTLINE FOR A FRIENDLY EAR
24 HOURS A DAY

"What a crock," Alex mumbled, stomping past it. When she got to her door, she pivoted sharply, backtracked down the hall, and squinted again at the flyer.

She pulled the flyer from the wall and tucked it down into the pocket of her robe. She'd have to think about this a little. It might be nice to have somebody to talk to. Somebody who hadn't known her since grade school. Somebody who hadn't known her as a college student. Somebody who didn't think she was a drunk and maybe even a tramp.

The Thetas were supposed to be her friends, she reflected as she shut and locked the door to her room. She should get her face made up, put on her clothes, and hurry over to Theta House now. They probably needed help getting things ready for the dinner tonight.

Alex sat down heavily on the bed. Who was she kidding? The awful truth was that her "sisters" weren't really her friends. There wasn't one of them she could turn to for comfort. And it wasn't all their fault, either. During the giddy weeks of her relationship with Mark, she had made him her whole life. The girls and their activities had been way down on her list of priorities.

Todd wasn't really her friend either. He was more like a partner in crime.

Elizabeth?

Alex thought back to the first weeks of college, when she'd been so full of herself and her romance with Mark. She felt her cheeks flush as she remembered the way she'd practically gone out of her way to antagonize and alienate her best friend from high school. She'd even gotten a perverse thrill from seeing Elizabeth have such a hard time adjusting to school. After that, Alex could hardly expect Elizabeth to give her a shoulder to cry on.

Nope. The way she saw it, these days she had only one friend.

She reached under the bed and groped around until she found it. Her hand closed over the neck of a bottle. "There you are. Looks like it's just you and me, *friend*."

Alex poured an inch of the clear liquid into an empty water glass next to her bed. Then she put the glass to her lips, bent back her head, and drank.

Bruce leaned against a tree and brushed his hair out of his face with his free hand. His other arm was wrapped around Lila's shoulders, and her head was snuggled in the hollow of his shoulder.

Talk about weird! he thought. *If somebody had told me last week that I'd be sitting here with my arm around Lila Fowler, I would have told them they were crazy.*

Bruce and Lila had squabbled, competed, and argued since they were children. When he'd heard that she was staying in Italy instead of enrolling at SVU, Bruce had been relieved that she wouldn't be around to try to upstage his position of money and power.

Of course, since she'd been back, Lila had made more of an impression on her fellow students than even Bruce had anticipated. People thought that being a young and wealthy widow gave Lila an aura of romance and sophistication.

Bruce had secretly thought it was kind of shocking and low class for a girl to marry the summer after she graduated from high school. But glancing down at her face, he couldn't help smiling.

Trust Lila to do the thing with maximum

splash. She hadn't just married some ordinary Joe Blow high school sweetheart. She had married the Count di Mondicci, a young, handsome, and incredibly rich man from one of the oldest families in Europe. They had been married hardly any time at all when he tragically died in a Jet-Ski accident. After that, Lila had returned to Sweet Valley.

No doubt about it; Lila Fowler was one in a million. But Bruce had never had any romantic thoughts about her—until now.

Something about being on their own, unarmed, and pitted against nature was turning them into better people. Maybe this was what life was really supposed to be. Maybe he and Lila were living out some weird destiny reserved only for them.

Take away the money, the cars, and the clothes, and they were just two young healthy people surviving in a primordial world. Tarzan and Jane. Adam and Eve.

Involuntarily his eyes traveled the length of her exposed leg. He couldn't help noting the shapely calf, the fine bones of her knee, the firm thigh.

It was very distracting.

He forced his eyes away and scanned the woods, looking for signs of danger.

Lila stirred, and Bruce gazed down at her face. Her lips looked red against her porcelain complexion.

As red as apples. As red as strawberries. All of a sudden, he felt an overpowering urge to kiss her.

"Bruce?"

"Yes?" It was only by exercising superhuman effort that he was able to refrain from touching his lips to hers.

She was wonderful.

She was beautiful.

She was sexy.

She was . . .

"Did you reload the flare gun?" she asked in a petulant tone.

. . . a nag. "You've asked me that five times," he responded, loosening his grip around her shoulders.

"And all five times you said you were going to do it. Did you?"

Bruce clenched his teeth. He wasn't about to admit that he'd forgotten. "Yeah," he answered. "Of course. You don't have to nag me every second."

"Who's nagging?" Lila demanded, sitting up.

"You are," Bruce replied, removing his arm altogether and straightening his back.

"Since when is asking someone if they've taken the logical steps toward saving their own life—*nagging*?"

"Since the fifth time you asked. You know, I'm

38

not a kid," Bruce said. "I'm a man. That means I don't need to be reminded about something five times."

She turned away impatiently and the cloth of her sweatpants fell away, revealing even more tanned, firm thigh. Bruce felt a curious melting sensation around his heart.

Get a grip, Patman, he ordered himself. *Don't be a jerk. That's Lila. Lila Fowler. A spoiled brat who's always looking for some way to put you down. The isolation is making you nuts. A couple of seconds ago, you were actually thinking that Lila Fowler was the most beautiful, sexy . . .*

Lila flexed her leg and her thigh muscle stood out in high relief.

Who wouldn't start thinking like a jerk with a leg like that stretched along the ground in front of him? He closed his eyes. It was too hard to think while looking at Lila's leg.

When he opened his eyes again, Lila looked off in the distance and flipped her hair back off her shoulder. She obviously had no idea that her leg was driving him nuts.

If he told her to cover it up, she'd just laugh and make fun of him. Was there some way of solving this problem and maintaining what was left of his dignity?

Abruptly he jumped up and ran to the plane.

"Where are you going?" Lila yelled.

Bruce began rummaging around the back of the plane. The guy who had sold him the Cessna had been a real outdoors enthusiast, and there was all kinds of miscellaneous gear and apparel stuffed in the back and under the seats.

"What are you looking for?" Lila demanded.

Bingo! Bruce thought. "Long underwear!" he answered happily, holding up a pair of beige long johns. He gave Lila a sympathetic smile. "The temperature's probably going to drop fifteen degrees over the next couple of hours," he said. "You're going to be cold. Why don't you go ahead and put these on?"

Lila stood, crossed her arms over her chest, and slowly circled him, eyeing the long underwear. "Not exactly what you'd call *couture* survival togs," she commented.

He examined the cleaning tags. "Hey! These johns are top-of-the-line combed cotton. And if I were standing there with one side of my pants ripped off, I wouldn't be turning up my nose at a pair of nice, warm long johns. Now put 'em on."

She reached out and took them with the tips of her fingers—like she was doing him a big favor. "Anything you say," she said sarcastically, heading toward the shelter of the cockpit.

As he watched her walk away, he couldn't help thinking what a great shape she had. Bruce ground his teeth in frustration. "For my sake, I hope those long johns make you look terrible," he muttered.

Chapter
Three

"Yo, Watts! Welcome back."

Elizabeth turned and smiled at the good-looking senior tackle who was enthusiastically ruffling the top of Tom's hair.

"How ya doin', Terry," Tom said, reaching out his own long arm and ruffling Terry's hair right back.

"Doin' okay." Terry grinned. He smoothed his hair and gave Elizabeth a smiling nod. "We miss you this year," he said, turning back to Tom.

There was a big crowd in the parking lot for the tailgate picnic, and Tom tightened his grasp on Elizabeth's hand. "You guys don't need me," he bantered. "The team was solid and you looked great out there. I just hope there were some scouts in the stands today."

"You and me both, pal."

The milling crowd surged between the two men, making further conversation impossible. Terry waved. "Talk to you later."

"Tom! Glad you're here, man." A hand reached out and slapped him on the shoulder. But whoever it was disappeared into the crowd before Tom or Elizabeth could respond. Tom pulled Elizabeth closer and put his arm around her.

"Looks like you've still got a lot of friends in the world of college football," Elizabeth said.

Tom nodded, and she saw him swallow hard. He'd started his freshman year as one of the greatest college athletes Sweet Valley University had ever seen. The scouts were following his every move. His picture had been in the sports section of ten major newspapers.

Everybody in the world had been in love with Tom Watts, he had explained to her once over several cups of coffee. "Everybody, including Tom Watts," she remembered him saying bitterly.

Not content with the adulation and admiration of his public, Tom had pressured his family into making the long trip from Colorado to see him in an important game. Instead of arriving in Sweet Valley, his whole family had died in a horrible car accident.

After that, Tom dropped out of college athletics. He had been too traumatized. Too heartbroken.

And convinced that his own ego had killed the people he loved most. He'd also decided that life was too short and uncertain to waste chasing a ball.

His coach hadn't been too happy about his choice. And neither had some of his teammates. But Tom had been adamant. Up until today he had followed sports from a distance, avoiding the games, the rallies, and all the pregame and postgame parties that went along with them.

"Hey! There's Watts!" a voice shouted.

"Tom! Tom! Come sit over here." Two guys standing in the back of a truck waved, motioning him over.

"On the way back," Tom promised. He seemed pleased to be receiving such friendly greetings. It was out of character, and Elizabeth couldn't help directing a surprised glance at his face. Maybe his wounds were finally beginning to heal.

Like her, he must have been finding it difficult to remain immune to the infectious enthusiasm and good cheer that had surrounded them from the moment they took their seats in the stadium.

The home team had won. But it had been a close game and suspenseful from the start. Even Elizabeth, who didn't usually get excited about football, had been on her feet screaming encouragement.

"So where's your sister?" Tom shouted over the general noise. "And when are you going to inspect James Montgomery?"

Elizabeth laughed. "I'm not here to *inspect* him," she retorted.

"No?" Tom took her hand and pulled her away from the crowd. "I had the distinct impression that she wanted us to come . . . *you* to come," he amended, "for the express purpose of checking this guy out. And given Jessica's track record, I don't blame her for wanting the official Elizabeth Wakefield seal of approval."

Elizabeth knew Tom was teasing, but she couldn't help realizing that a seal of approval wasn't such a bad idea. Her twin's short, passionate courtship by and marriage to Michael McAllery had left Jessica more than a little leery of men. Mike had been older, wilder, a little dangerous, and ultimately a terrible mistake.

In contrast, James Montgomery was a sophomore, premed, and a football star. Elizabeth had seen him a few times, but all she really knew about him was his jersey number. That number had done all right, she thought. She'd watched James Montgomery, a.k.a. number fifty-two, score four touchdowns, including the final, game-winning point.

"Something tells me we're going to find

Jessica's football hero over there." Tom pointed to a large crowd of people, mostly girls, who seemed to be gathered around someone. A familiar figured emerged from the crowd and hurried toward them.

"Liz! Tom!" Jessica cried. She held out her hands. "I thought you'd never get here. Come on." She took Elizabeth and Tom each by the hand, but Tom pulled back.

"I'll stay here and maybe catch up with some people," he said. "You go on."

Before Elizabeth could protest, a group of guys closed in around Tom. Elizabeth let Jessica drag her into James's admiring crowd and followed while Jessica elbowed her way to the front. She pointed proudly at James. "Liz, this is James. James, this is my sister, Elizabeth."

James turned to Elizabeth and smiled warmly. "I'm glad to finally get a chance to talk to you." He took her small hand in his and shook it.

"Congratulations on your win," Elizabeth said.

"*Our* win," James corrected gently. "It takes a whole team to win a game."

Elizabeth thought that was a nice thing to hear. A lot of jocks tended to act like they had been the only guy on the field, court, or track.

James put his arm around Jessica's shoulders. "I guess you know you have a pretty wonderful sister?"

"So I've been told."

"Mainly by me." Jessica laughed.

James chuckled—a smooth, rich, deep-in-the-chest laugh that inspired confidence.

"James!" a wide-eyed freshman reporter interrupted. "Mind if I ask you a couple of questions about SVU's game strategy?"

"Excuse me for a second, will you?" James asked Elizabeth. "I really need to answer some of Rhonda's questions. She's got a deadline." He smiled. "I know you know what those are like. I've heard about your journalism career."

Rhonda wasn't the only reporter present. Pretty soon several young men and women were peppering James with questions. Slowly but surely, Elizabeth was squeezed out of the circle surrounding him.

Oh, well, Elizabeth thought as she made her way back toward Tom. *At least we got to say hello. And I didn't see any horns or hooves.*

"So, what did you think?" Tom asked when she reached his side.

"Polished. Polite. Intelligent. And definitely a gentleman," Elizabeth responded promptly.

"Just like me," Tom joked.

Elizabeth kissed his cheek. "There's nobody like you," she said affectionately.

*　　　*　　　*

He couldn't believe it. Couldn't believe she would foul her lips on the stubbly chin of a low-brow television-tabloid hack like Tom Watts.

Elizabeth's eyes turned in his direction, and William White backed up into the shadows of the oak trees that were clumped around the terrace across from the stadium parking lot.

He had gotten a good clear look at her. Had she gotten a good clear look at him?

Fool, he cursed himself. In his eagerness to see her, he had allowed himself to become careless. It would be unfortunate—for him and for her—if she spotted him before he was ready to reveal himself.

She feared him now. Well, that was reasonable. A few months ago, he had tried to murder her. It was regrettable that their relationship had resulted in such an unfortunate contretemps, but he hoped to make her see that at the time, he'd had no choice. She had discovered that he was the president of an influential secret society. What could he do? Exposure would have proved disastrous.

Did prove disastrous, he mentally amended, feeling a flash of anger surge behind his eyeballs.

He forced the anger down. That was all in the past now. Soon, very soon, he would explain things to her so that she would understand. So that she would forgive. So that she would join and assist him in his new schemes. And if she wouldn't . . .

William glanced down at his watch. He didn't have much time to get back to the loony bin, where he was supposedly a prisoner. The place was a nightmare—thank God he'd more or less managed to arrange on his own when he would and would not be there.

William cast another look in Elizabeth's direction and was relieved to see that she was chatting easily with Tom Watts, clearly undisturbed by anything she might have seen. Only by force of will was he able to drag his eyes from her beautiful face.

He was going to have to move very cautiously. Very carefully. There was no margin for error. One clumsy move on his part and it would be over.

He would have to be more patient. Exercise more self-restraint. She was his goddess. And he didn't want to have to kill her.

At least not yet.

Jessica clasped the little gold megaphone on a chain and arranged it at the neck of her sweater with the big SVH on it.

It was fun having on her high school cheerleading uniform—and she figured it was a great costume for James Montgomery's date.

As she approached Theta House she quickened her step. Jessica had told Isabella Ricci, her close friend at the sorority, that she wanted to meet her at the house for dinner—but she hadn't told her she was planning to mow down Alison Quinn.

Jessica's pulse raced a little—with anger, anticipation, and a slight bit of nervousness. Some of the girls were still friendly, but a lot of them were giving her a wide berth these days—waiting to see what happened with the investigation.

Jessica squared her shoulders and set her face in a determined smile. She was prepared to receive a mixed reception. But how should she play it? Go in like she owned the world? Or keep her head low and not draw any attention to herself until the time was right?

She paused, watching a pair of giggling Thetas in green Martian costumes hurry up the steps of the house. Behind them Isabella bounded up the stairs, giving their shoulders a teasing push and saying something that made them all laugh even harder as they disappeared inside the front door.

She'd play it supremely confident, Jessica decided. Totally composed. She would glide in as if she had every right to be there—which she did. And by the end of dinner tonight, she thought grimly, the whole sorority was going to know it.

Jessica began waving her pom-poms as she

bounded up the front steps of Theta House and into the large front parlor. She did a one-handed cartwheel, then sank down into a split.

"All right, Jessica!" shouted Kimberly Schyler, the Theta treasurer.

Isabella stood back and eyed Jessica from head to foot. "Perfect." She sighed. "I wish I had kept my high school cheerleading outfit. It makes a great costume."

"Me too," Denise Waters moaned, breaking away from the group of girls in the hall to join their conversation. "We could have said we were a squad."

"Whose idea was it to make the postgame bash a costume party?" Jessica asked. "Not that I'm complaining."

"Probably yours," Denise teased. "You probably just wanted a chance to wear your cheerleader uniform one more time. And I have to admit, it looks amazing on you."

"You guys don't look so bad yourself."

Isabella was dressed as a harlequin clown, complete with a three-cornered hat. And Denise wore an elegant black cat suit with delicate black whiskers penciled along her exquisitely hollow cheeks.

The girls laughed, and Jessica gazed affectionately around her. Her eyes rested on Isabella's smiling face. Isabella had never stopped being a faithful and loyal supporter. Even when she disapproved of Mike. Even when *everybody* disapproved of Mike.

Jessica's disastrous and scandal-ridden marriage had made some of the Thetas determined to expel her from their ranks. And her "arrest" by campus security for stealing Professor Martin's book had been the last straw for many of the girls.

Jessica understood that Isabella's support was the reason she was receiving such a warm welcome now.

"Jessica, *darling*," a senior member oozed. "I saw you with James Montgomery." She kissed her fingers with the gesture of a connoisseur. "Nice. Very nice."

"He's a doll," said Gloria Abel, a petite redhead, as she hurried into the dining room from the kitchen with a huge salad bowl.

"Except when he drinks," Courtney Long said knowingly.

Jessica felt her brows knit in confusion. "What are you talking about? James doesn't—"

"What are you doing here?" a cold voice interrupted.

Immediately the happy chatter and giggles died and the crowded room was silent.

Jessica turned slowly toward the unfriendly face of Alison Quinn. One look at Alison's stuck-up, cold, fish-eyed expression turned Jessica's heart to stone, and she relished the prospect of humiliating her. "As a matter of fact, Alison," she said in a conversational voice, "I was hoping to run into you."

Alison's brows rose in surprise. "Oh?"

"Yes. I wanted you to be the first to know. Professor Martin is dropping his charges. I'm in the clear."

Isabella's arms were the first ones around her neck.

"Jessica, I'm thrilled!" Courtney crowed.

"You're a baby Theta again," Denise said happily.

"Not so fast," Alison barked so ferociously that every head snapped in her direction.

"What's wrong?" Denise asked.

"It doesn't matter if the charges were dropped," Alison insisted. "She didn't complete the dare. She didn't bring us the book."

Jessica's heart leapt. She couldn't have wished for a better setup.

She took a few measured steps in Alison's direction, then stopped and looked her straight in the eye. "How could I," she asked sweetly, "when you called campus security and told them exactly when I'd arrive at Professor Martin's office?"

There were several sharp gasps and a stunned silence.

"Is that true?" Kimberly asked Alison.

Alison's face turned an ugly red. "Of course it's not true. She's lying."

"The whole book-stealing idea was yours," Courtney said slowly.

"I didn't mean steal it forever. I just meant for her to borrow it." Alison's tone was biting.

"Still," Isabella said thoughtfully. "The dare was your idea. And if you *had* been trying to set Jessica up, you figured out a great way. And you got all of us to go along with you."

"You're jumping to conclusions," Alison argued.

"We are jumping to conclusions," said Tina Chai, a pretty sophomore, in an undecided tone.

"To the *right* conclusions," Denise asserted dogmatically.

The room erupted with arguments, accusations, counter-accusations, and even tears. The noise and the tension built and swirled until Jessica felt as if she were at the center of a hurricane. She fought the impulse to dive under a wing chair and protect the back of her head from flying debris.

"Quiet!" an authoritative voice thundered.

Immediately the din ceased.

Magda Helperin, the tall, dignified president of the Thetas, stood on a coffee table. "We can't let something like this split us apart." Her eyes swept the room and rested briefly on every face. "Basically, this boils down to Jessica's word against Alison's. I think we're going to have to settle this with a house vote. We'll do it tomorrow. In the meantime, I want us all to remember that we're sisters."

Her eyes bored in on Jessica's, and Jessica swallowed nervously. A house vote was a pretty major event. It was like a trial with no appeal. A decision would be made, and that would be that.

A house vote could turn out to be a show of support for Jessica. Or it could mean she was blackballed.

Chapter Four

Creak!

The door opened just a crack, and Maia's suspicious face peeped out. "Elizabeth!" The wary look left her face, and Maia opened the door. "What are you doing here?" Her eyes inspected Elizabeth from head to toe. "And why are you dressed up like a scarecrow?"

"I'm going to the costume party at Zeta house, and I was hoping you'd come with me."

"You're going to a fraternity party?" Maia repeated in a surprised tone.

Elizabeth grinned and straightened her burlap tunic. "I know I'm not the frat type, but I just can't resist a costume party." She shrugged. "What can I say? I'm a hopeless dork."

She watched Maia's lips curve into a smile and felt glad she had come by. Elizabeth stepped into

Maia's room. After the tailgate picnic her mind had wandered back to Maia and her unhappy mood. The campus atmosphere was so festive and upbeat that she had decided to see if she could lure Maia out and lift her spirits.

"A costume party. Hmmm?" Maia gestured at her own attire. Flannel nightgown. Oversized robe. And fuzzy slippers. "Think I could pass for the Queen of Sloth?"

Elizabeth shook her head. "No. And I don't think you should even try. I think you should rig up some outrageous and sexy costume and strut your stuff." She grabbed the loose sleeve of Maia's robe. "I'm the last one to give out fashion advice, but you've been wearing a lot of this big and baggy stuff lately. Have you gained ten pounds that nobody knows about?"

Maia smiled thinly and pulled her robe around her protectively. "Nope. Lost a few, as a matter of fact."

Elizabeth sat down at Maia's desk chair and studied her friend's face. She was such a pretty girl when she lost the tense frown she had been wearing lately.

"What are you staring at?"

"I was wondering what a fun, intelligent woman like you is doing hanging out in the dorm on a Saturday night."

"Look who's asking," Maia squeaked. "You told me you turned into a total dorm potato early in the year."

Elizabeth laughed. "I know, I know. I did stay home a lot for a while. But that was because I felt fat, ugly, unpopular, and dull."

"Well, maybe I'm feeling a little fat, ugly, unpopular, and dull myself."

"You just said you'd lost a few pounds."

"So I'm feeling *thin*, ugly, unpopular, and dull," Maia responded. Her voice was light, but there was a faint note of hostility that even she must have heard. She immediately dropped her eyes. "Sorry," she mumbled.

"I'm not here looking for an apology," Elizabeth said gently. "I'm here to find out what's wrong. And to help if I can."

This time, Maia's smile seemed genuine. "You're a nice person."

There was a long pause, and Elizabeth waited. Obviously something was on Maia's mind that she didn't want to talk about. If she would just confide in Elizabeth, maybe they could talk it through.

But Maia just stared stubbornly at the floor.

Elizabeth didn't know quite what to do. She didn't want to pry. But she saw a lot of herself in Maia, and she knew that if somebody didn't pull her up out of this hole, she was going to burrow down in her misery like a groundhog.

"I wish you'd get dressed and come to the party with me," she said, trying to make her voice sound coaxing without sounding patronizing. "Tom's supposed to meet me there, but I hate going in by myself—and I'll bet he'll take us both out for something chocolate after the party."

Maia frowned. "Tell Tom I'm sorry about that 'jocks' remark. It really wasn't aimed at him."

Elizabeth stood up. "Tell him yourself. Show him you want to be friends by making him the only man there with *two* dates."

Maia let out a reluctant laugh. "Okay, okay. You're twisting my arm, but maybe you're right. A night out will do me good. I'll go—but I'm not wearing a costume," she insisted.

No? Elizabeth wondered as she watched Maia pull a huge pair of jeans and an extra-large, long-sleeved sweatshirt out of her drawer. She pressed her lips together firmly. It was none of her business, so she wasn't going to say a word. If Maia wanted to disguise a beautiful figure in baggy jeans and a sweatshirt, that was up to her.

"So where's Jessica?" Maia asked as the two girls made their way through the throng of people in the backyard of Zeta house. Elizabeth was glad she had pressed Maia to come. Her eyes had a little of the snap and sparkle Elizabeth had been used to seeing. "She's here somewhere," Elizabeth answered. "With her new boyfriend," she added.

"Who's the new boyfriend?" Maia shouted in Elizabeth's ear as the volume on the music was cranked even louder.

Elizabeth stood on tiptoe and peered over a couple of hundred heads until she saw Jessica's familiar blond head next to James's dark-haired one. "There they are."

Maia stood on her tiptoes too. "Where?"

Elizabeth pointed toward the crowd that had gathered around the metal washtub full of ice and beers and sodas. "There."

As she watched, James put one arm around Jessica and hugged her to him. Jessica smiled happily up at him, and he bent to kiss her.

"So what do you think?" Elizabeth asked. "Is that a guy you could take home to meet the folks, or what?"

There was no answer from Maia.

"Maia?"

Silence.

"Maia?" Elizabeth looked around for Maia, but she was gone.

A couple of guys began horsing around behind Elizabeth. One of them bumped her, and her soda cup turned over and splashed her burlap tunic.

"Sorry," the guy said immediately. "Want me to get you a napkin or something?"

Elizabeth shook her head. "No sweat. I think burlap is washable."

The guy laughed and Elizabeth moved on, weaving through the thick crowd in search of Maia.

"Looking for me?" a voice at her elbow asked a few minutes later.

Elizabeth turned and saw Tom smiling at her. "Actually, I was looking for Maia."

"Maia?" Tom frowned. "I saw her going out as I came in."

"What? Where was she going?"

"To her dorm, I guess. She was running. Said she wasn't feeling well and couldn't stop to talk."

"That's crazy. Three minutes ago she was standing right here and . . ."

Tom's face was a study in boredom.

"Never mind," she said. It was clear that Tom's mind was somewhere else. And whatever was bugging Maia, she seemed determined to keep it to herself. "This place isn't doing it for you, is it?"

Tom ran his hand over his jaw. "Nope. It really isn't. Fraternity parties just aren't my thing."

"Looks like costume parties aren't either," she said, glancing at his jeans, button-down shirt, and sneakers.

"I'm in costume. I'm dressed as a fire-breathing, tough-as-nails broadcast journalist."

"But you *are* a fire-breathing, tough-as-nails broadcast journalist."

"Only by day," he said. "By night . . ." He put his arms around her and pulled her close. "By night I'm . . ."

"Batman?" she guessed.

"A blood-sucking vampire. Wanna go to the beach?"

"The beach? Hmmm. Can you be trusted?"

"Nope."

"Good," she said with a giggle. "Let's go."

"Well, well, well. Long time, no see. We missed you at the dinner." Isabella fell into step beside Alex as she hurried up the sidewalk toward Zeta house. Alex wobbled a little on her spiked heels as she tried to keep pace with Isabella's long-legged strides. But it was hard in her tight, twenties-style flapper costume.

Alex nervously adjusted the straps of her dress. "I had a lot of homework, and then the phone rang. I just sort of lost track of the time and . . ." Alex babbled on in flustered confusion, making excuse after excuse for her absence at the game and the Theta dinner.

"I wasn't nagging you," Isabella said pleasantly. "You don't need to make excuses. At least not to me."

"I should talk to Magda, I guess," Alex mumbled.

"It would probably be a good idea. Nobody's seen you around Theta House in a while, and I think people are wondering if you're thinking of depledging."

"Do the girls *want* me to depledge?"

Isabella adjusted her tricorner hat. "No," she said after a moment's hesitation. "Of course not."

That moment's hesitation spoke volumes.

"Is there anything I should know?" Alex asked quietly. She stepped back a little. She was afraid if she got too close, Isabella would smell the shot of vodka that had gotten her up and out of her room.

She had brushed her teeth twice and gargled with mouthwash, but she could still taste the slightly etherish, unpleasant alcohol aftertaste.

Isabella pursed her lips and looked around to make sure that none of the passing partygoers were watching them. "Look," she said in a low voice. "I'm not the rules committee or the house mother or the chaplain or anything else. But since you asked me, I'll tell you what I think. For your own sake, you should probably clean up your act a little."

Isabella wasn't telling her anything she didn't know already. But it was still hard to hear it stated so plainly. Alex swallowed hard, determined not to cry. She had worked too hard on her hair and makeup to let tears make her look worse than she already did after last night's binge.

"It's really hard for everybody on campus to agree on what's a reasonable drinking policy," Isabella continued in a matter-of-fact tone. "And there's a lot of confusion in our sorority. But when a girl starts . . . well . . . *drawing attention to her drinking* . . ." She trailed off and shrugged. "What can I say? That girl is making her problem the sorority's problem. And frankly, the sorority just doesn't know what to do about it."

"Meaning they'll kick me out."

Isabella shook her head. "Probably not. What would more likely happen is that you would just start to feel less and less welcome."

Alex nodded unhappily. "I get it. And when I feel unwelcome enough, I'll depledge."

Isabella's large, dark eyes were open and friendly. But her air of self-possession and sophistication made Alex feel totally awkward and inadequate.

The girl in front of her was everything a Theta was supposed to be. And Alex was everything the Thetas despised. She blushed with shame, and her eyelashes fluttered as she fought tears of humiliation.

Isabella put her hand on Alex's shoulder and shook it gently. "Hey, hey!" she admonished gently. "Don't break down on me. I'm not saying this is going to happen today or tomorrow or next week. It may not happen at all. I'm just telling you that I've seen it happen."

"I feel so embarrassed," Alex whispered.

"Don't be embarrassed. Get on the stick and launch operation damage control. Quit moping around over Mark Gathers. He's gone. He's history. Find a new guy. Start over. He didn't die. It's not like you're obligated to observe a period of mourning."

A little smile began to play around Alex's lips.

"That smile tells me these are not new ideas to you," Isabella teased.

"There is a guy I sort of . . ."

"Sort of what?"

"Sort of like."

"Who is he?"

"I'd rather not talk about it. It's ridiculous to even think about, and . . ."

"Why is it ridiculous?" Isabella asked with a soft smile.

Alex just shook her head. How could she say she had a semi-crush on Noah Pearson just because he had a friendly smile?

"You don't have to tell me," Isabella said quickly. "I'm just glad you're thinking about tomorrow instead of crying over yesterday."

"Isabella!" Denise Waters stood on the front porch of Zeta house and waved. "Where have you been?"

"You guys ate and ran. Somebody had to clean up the house after the dinner," Isabella called back in a jovial scold.

Denise laughed. "Better you than me," she joked. "You guys come in. They're about to judge the costumes."

"You go on," Alex said. "I'll catch up in a minute." She held up her evening bag. "I want to check my lipstick and hair before making my big entrance."

"Okay. I'll see you inside."

Isabella trotted off, and Alex pulled out her compact for a quick examination. In the soft light of the early evening, she looked fine. Better than fine, really. She looked pretty.

She shut her compact with a snap. Tonight she wasn't going to have anything to drink except a soda. Isabella was right. It was time to make a fresh start—as of right now, this minute.

Her heart fluttered a little when she pictured Noah Pearson. She'd heard him mention in psychology class that he would be at the party. He was so nice. He was probably the kind of guy who would be receptive to being approached by a girl.

Alex nervously fluffed her hair. Would she have the guts?

She forced her quaking hands to be still and lifted her chin. Of course she had the guts. All she had to do was walk up to Noah, give him a two-hundred-kilowatt smile, and start a conversation.

About what?

About anything. "So tell me, Noah. Are you planning to major in psychology?" she practiced.

She repeated the question over and over as she climbed the steps to Zeta house, entered the raucous party, and began looking around.

Several couples were dancing in the living room, and a crowd had gathered in the den, where several people with elaborate costumes were being judged.

She was moving slowly, gently elbowing her way toward the kitchen, when her heart gave a thump.

There he was. Noah Pearson. He was leaning against a counter in the kitchen and talking to some other guy.

"So tell me, Noah. Are you planning to major in psychology?" she rehearsed one last time.

Alex pulled the corners of her mouth back into a wide smile that showed both rows of teeth. She threw back her shoulders. She let her arms hang and swing slightly at her sides.

She felt cool. Confident. Secure. She tried to imagine that she was moving inside Isabella Ricci's lithe and graceful body.

He'd spotted her. She could tell from the almost imperceptible smile he gave her. His lips were moving, and he was still talking to the red-headed guy, but his eyes were focused on Alex. He leaned slightly in her direction, poised to return her greeting.

"So tell me, Noah. Are you planning to . . . *whoaaaaa!*" she broke off with a shriek as her heel skidded across a wet puddle on the floor. She lurched forward with her arms cartwheeling.

"Hey!" the redheaded guy exclaimed as Alex bumped his shoulder and then fell on Noah's chest.

Several girls cried out in alarm when the cup in Noah's hand went flying. A few were splashed with a spray of icy-cold cherry soda.

Noah's large hands reached out and gripped Alex's arms before she could fall to the floor.

"Are you okay?" she heard him ask as he

hoisted her up. Alex's feet skittered as she tried to keep her balance.

Finally she managed to stand up on her own. "I'm sorry," she sputtered. "I don't know how . . . I was just wal—"

Noah gave her arm a friendly squeeze and opened his mouth to speak.

"Lay off the beer, why don't you?" a dark-haired guy muttered as several people hurried to the sink to wipe the red liquid off their clothes.

Alex could almost hear the blood rushing to her face. She had never felt so mortified in her whole life. Noah had obviously overheard the remark and probably everybody else had, too.

"I'm sorry," she said again, pulling away from Noah's grasp. She practically ran toward the back door and was grateful for the huge, rowdy crowd that milled around in the backyard.

She found herself moving in the direction of the beer keg and lining up behind a group of guys. The guys immediately stepped back politely. "Ladies first," a nice-looking freshman from her English class said. He took a cup, stuck it under the keg until it was full, and presented it to Alex with a flourish. "Thank you," she murmured, still so embarrassed she could hardly look him in the eye.

She lifted the cup to her lips and then paused.

Hadn't she decided she wasn't going to drink tonight?

Oh, well. *I'll start my fresh start tomorrow,* she thought miserably.

Bruce rubbed his hands together in front of the fire. "I still don't think we need to be so careful about conserving your matches," he said to Lila. "But I have to admit, you must have been some Girl Scout! I couldn't light a fire without a match if my life depended on it." Bruce could hear reluctant admiration in his voice.

"I didn't learn that in Girl Scouts. I learned it at one of those high-powered, high-priced corporate survival weekends. That's the really trendy thing for businesspeople these days. I guess they figure if you can learn to survive in the Bolivian jungle, you can learn to survive in a boardroom."

Bruce chuckled, and Lila fed a few more twigs into the tiny, smoldering fire. "My dad signed a bunch of his executives up for it and I went along for a laugh." She leaned over and blew on the glowing embers. "We spent eight days in the Bolivian jungle with five of his vice presidents and two of the top survival guides in the business. We learned to build a fire, set a snare, find water, track. All that stuff."

"Sounds like a blast," Bruce said. "If we ever

get back to civilization, I might sign up for it myself—in case I'm ever lost in the wilderness again."

Lila sat down next to him and smiled. The light from the blaze lit her features with a golden light. She looked like a painting, he decided. A beautiful, seventeenth-century Madonna wearing long johns.

She stretched out her legs and flexed her expensively booted feet. Much to Bruce's dismay, the long johns hadn't disguised any of Lila's lovely curves. If anything, they emphasized them.

"I found these in the pocket of my flight jacket," he said, pulling a partially eaten packet of peanut butter crackers from his back pocket. "It's not Bolivian possum," he said apologetically. "But it's food."

"I'm not complaining," Lila said, eagerly snatching the two peanut butter crackers he held out. She crammed them in her mouth and chewed ravenously, not bothering to take small bites and obviously not worried about what he thought.

It was oddly attractive. Maybe because he had never seen Lila without all her pretensions and affectations. Minute by minute she was looking more like a real woman.

He handed her the bottle of water. She drank

thirstily, then wiped the back of her mouth with her hand, just missing a tiny crumb along the line of her full lower lip.

"What are you looking at?" she asked. "Why are you staring?"

He tried to drag his eyes away, but he couldn't.

"Bruce?" she prompted. "What are you looking at?"

"Uh . . . you have something on your mouth," he said.

She lifted a finger and wiped delicately at the edge of her mouth. "Here?"

As hard as he tried, Bruce couldn't seem to look at anything but her lips. "No," he said hoarsely. "Right there." He reached forward to remove the crumb that clung to her lower lip and then . . . somehow . . . she was in his arms.

"Lila," he breathed against her cheek. She turned her face toward his, and when their lips met, a thrill of excitement raced up Bruce's spine and exploded somewhere behind his brain. No woman had ever felt quite so alive in his arms. No woman had ever made him feel quite so male.

She felt it too. All the passion and excitement he was feeling. He could tell from the ragged, shuddering breath that escaped her as his arms tightened around her waist.

There was a distant whisking sound, and Lila broke away and tensed. "Listen. I hear something."

"Who cares?" he moaned, pulling her back toward him.

But she planted her hand firmly on his chest and pushed. "It's a helicopter!"

The whisking sound was louder now, and Bruce cocked his head to catch the sound.

The prospect of rescue finally, and successfully, pushed Lila and her leg to the back of Bruce's brain. No doubt about it, that was a helicopter. A helicopter that probably belonged to the national park rangers.

"Where's the flare gun?" Lila demanded as he got to his feet. "Get it. Quick!"

Bruce lurched toward their pile of provisions and tools and tripped over the fire. The delicately burning twigs scattered in every direction and flickered out in the dirt.

"Oh, no!" he cried.

"It doesn't matter!" Lila shouted, rushing past him and darting for the flare gun. "We're about to be rescued!"

The noise was getting louder and louder as the helicopter neared their location.

Lila gave him a euphoric smile just before lifting the flare gun and pulling the trigger.

. . . again.

. . . and again.

. . . and again.

The sound of the helicopter receded as it flew away into the distance.

"You idiot!" she shrieked, throwing the useless flare gun on the ground. "You didn't reload it, did you? You liar. You moron!"

Bruce wished his legs were double jointed so he could kick himself in the head.

Alex was in the middle of an anti-conversation with a guy named Albert from her history class. He was tall, skinny, and blond. His ponytail bobbed back and forth as he swayed slightly. "I'm thinking of majoring in business," he repeated for about the fifteenth time. "What about you?" He lifted his beer cup to his mouth to drink and wound up pouring the beer over his chin. "Oops!" He pawed clumsily at the breast of his shirt, trying to wipe up the spill. "Shhorry."

Alex took a long drink of her own beer. How many was it now? Four? Five? She'd lost count. Enough to get good and drunk, though.

"I'm thinking of majoring in business," Albert repeated in a bleary, beery voice. "What about you?"

Alex wondered if it was even worth bothering to answer the question again. Neither one of them was going to remember many details about this conversation tomorrow morning.

Her head began to pound as the laughter and noise of a dozen conversations swirled around her. Increasingly the evening seemed to be taking on the aura of a nightmare. A dizzying montage of sights, sounds, and faces that had no connection to one another.

She shook her head, trying to focus. Without bothering to excuse herself, she backed away from Albert and took refuge in the dark shadows of the hedge that ran between Zeta house and Sigma house.

A sibilant buzzing sound beyond the hedge penetrated the fog that was closing in around her brain. Listening closely, she realized that the shrill, intense sounds were voices.

"What do you mean, she knows you were the tipster?" a male voice hissed. "How could she possibly know?"

"Who cares?" a second voice—female—asked bitterly. "She knows I turned her in. And she's more or less put two and two together. She's figured out the whole thing was a setup."

"Does she have any proof?" the male voice asked.

"Not as far as I know."

"Then it's just her word against yours. And nobody thinks Jessica's word is worth spit these days. She's got no credibility."

Alex stood up on her tiptoes and craned her neck to peer over the hedge. No wonder the voices sounded familiar. They belonged to Alison Quinn and Peter Wilbourne, the ex-president of the Sigmas and the only guy Alex knew who was as snobby and mean spirited as Alison Quinn.

Hmmmm. Very interesting. *I should probably make an effort to remember this,* she thought, desperately wishing her double vision would clear up. One Alison Quinn and Peter Wilbourne were enough. Two of each was really more than she could cope with.

She heard a hiccup at her shoulder, and a heavy hand tapped her on the back. "Hey, Alex. I wondered where you went."

Alex groaned. Even in the shadows, Albert had managed to find her.

"I'm thinking of majoring in business," he droned as she drained her glass. "How about . . ."

Alex didn't hear the rest. Standing on her toes had taken the last of her energy and concentration. Before Albert had a chance to finish his sentence, she turned and stumbled from the party. All she wanted to do was lay her head on her pillow and escape into sleep.

Chapter Five

"Go, Jess!"

"Go, James!"

Jessica threw back her head and laughed as James dipped her almost to the floor. Isabella had turned on some old big band music, and that was when Jessica discovered that James was not only a football hero, a straight-*A* student, and a hunk, he was also a great dancer.

The music came to an end, and the crowd around them burst into applause. Jessica felt a thrill of excitement. It was wonderful being in the limelight again.

All around her she saw friendly and admiring faces. A lot of them were Theta faces. She felt a sudden sag in her spirits. She was having such a good time, she had almost forgotten the earlier unpleasantness and the house vote that would take place tomorrow.

77

As the other couples returned to the dance floor, her eyes sought out Isabella and Denise. They were smiling and laughing. Jessica's spirits rose again. Why was she worrying? She still had her friends. And it looked like a lot of people were changing their minds about her. Things were going to work out fine. James gave her a squeeze. "Dancing makes me thirsty. I need a beer."

Another one? Jessica couldn't help thinking. James had started drinking beer as soon as they had arrived. It wasn't like he was drunk or anything, but she couldn't help remembering Courtney's earlier remark. *Except when he drinks!*

"You coming?"

"No, you go," Jessica said with a smile. "I want to talk to Isabella and Denise."

"I'll bring you back a soda," he promised.

James disappeared toward the back, and Jessica hurried to join her friends.

"Let's go out on the front porch," Isabella suggested.

"Is that kind of dancing as much fun as it looks?" Denise asked as the girls stepped out into the cool night air.

"When you've got a great partner, it almost feels like you're flying," Jessica answered.

"Speaking of which," Isabella remarked,

"where's our resident jet-setter? Do we have any idea when Lila is coming back?"

Jessica shook out her tangled hair. "She said she was going to a spa with her mother. They must be at some ashram-type place with no phones or TVs—otherwise I'd have heard from her."

"Maybe she met a new man," Isabella suggested. "And that's why we haven't heard from her."

That started a conversation about men, which led to a conversation about dates, which led to a conversation about clothes, which led to a conversation about men again.

Twenty minutes later Jessica realized that James still hadn't returned with her soda. She reluctantly broke away and stepped into the front hall, letting the screen door shut behind her with a bang.

She immediately flagged Bob Pitts, who brushed past her with a six-pack of beers. "Bob! Have you seen James?"

"James? He's upstairs," Bob answered.

"Upstairs?"

"Yeah! I was just up there and came down for fresh provisions."

"Thanks," Jessica said, putting her hand on the banister. She ran lightly up the steps behind him. What was James doing upstairs? And why hadn't he come back to find her on the porch?

She heard loud male laughter coming from the third-floor game room. When she reached the door, she froze.

Several guys were gathered around James, chanting and clapping in a rhythm that matched the bobbing of James's Adam's apple as he chugged a huge glass of beer.

When the glass was empty, he smacked his lips and smiled. He caught a glimpse of Jessica, and his eyes lit up. "Jessie!" he cried happily.

Jessica felt annoyance flare up inside her. James sounded totally out of it, and she hated being called Jessie.

He staggered in her direction. When he got within a foot of where she was standing, he abruptly grabbed her and bent her backward while he planted a rough kiss on her lips. His breath smelled strongly of alcohol. A knot grew in her stomach as a scene from the last fraternity party she'd gone to with James flashed before her. His kisses had gotten out of hand, and when she'd told him to stop, there had been a strange look in his eyes.

Jessica involuntarily turned her head away. "James! Cut it out."

James didn't even seem to notice her reaction. Neither did the other guys. They were busily popping open the cans of beer that Bob had brought upstairs.

"How's my Jessie?" he asked, pulling her up and then bending her back and swaying her from side to side. "Having a good time?"

Funny. Being lifted and pulled and swung around had been incredibly fun on the dance floor.

But now, it wasn't any fun at all.

Elizabeth watched the whitecaps of the waves as they foamed and broke in the moonlight. She had left her burlap tunic in the car and was wearing the T-shirt she'd had on underneath with one of Tom's large sweatshirts over it.

Her head rested on Tom's shoulder, and she sighed happily. She heard Tom's echoing sigh and lifted her face to receive his kiss.

Tom's lips brushed lightly against Elizabeth's and she fell back, melting into the sand. He rolled on top of her and covered her face with soft kisses.

The beach was dark, but the sand was still warm from the sun and it felt good against her back. Breezes from the ocean lifted the soft tendrils of hair around her face, and it was hard to tell whether it was the breeze or Tom's gentle fingers that caressed her face.

As his kisses became more passionate, so did hers. Her hand moved to the back of his neck.

81

Little by little, control was slipping away as they pressed their bodies together.

"You're beautiful," he whispered, placing his hand on her stomach. "So beautiful I can hardly believe you're real."

The words were simple and clichéd. But the feelings between them seemed so real and so right that Tom's declaration felt fresh and honest.

"I think you're beautiful too," she whispered back.

His fingers left a trail of goose bumps as they traveled upward. Elizabeth closed her eyes and sighed. She trusted Tom. Trusted him completely. He would never hurt her. Never use her. Never make her feel ashamed of her feelings. So why not keep going?

Because sex was sex and biology was biology, that's why. No matter how well intentioned Tom was, sex had consequences, and Elizabeth wasn't ready to take them. Elizabeth's mind started racing. She didn't want to get pregnant, and she sure didn't want AIDS or any other kind of sexually transmitted disease.

His hand moved over the cup of her bra.

"No," she said softly.

He pressed his lips more firmly against hers and reached around her back to unhook her bra.

Elizabeth turned her face away and tried to

break out of his embrace. But his lips followed hers. "Don't," she said again.

Tom's grip tightened, and he pressed his body down against her, pinning her to the sand.

"Stop it!" she shouted.

Immediately Tom took his hands off her and sat up. The note of anger and alarm in her voice seemed to have shocked him. His skin looked white in the moonlight.

There was anger, hurt, and contrition written all over his face, and Elizabeth had to bite back an apology. She wasn't going to apologize for exercising her right to say no. Not even to Tom.

She sat up and brushed the sand off her arms.

There was a long, awkward pause.

She could hear Tom breathing hard. "I'm sorry," he finally said in a subdued voice. "I didn't understand."

Elizabeth opened her mouth to answer, but no words came out. She was upset, but she couldn't think of a way to articulate why.

Tom reached around and rubbed the back of his neck. "Sometimes you say *no* when you mean *yes*. It gets confusing."

"That's not true!" Elizabeth protested.

"It is too. And I can't read your mind. So how do I know if you're saying no as in *no, I shouldn't* or no as in *no, I don't want to.*"

83

Maybe he had a point. Had she done that in the course of their relationship? She remembered a night not long ago when . . . Okay. Yeah. She had done that once or twice.

She stood up. "I think it's good that we're having this conversation," she said softly. "Because it's making me focus. Making me put my feelings into words. No means no. Okay. It's my body. My decision. And I don't owe you any explanations. Girls don't have to give reasons for saying no."

Tom raised his hands in a gesture of surrender. "Whatever you say. All I want is for us to get past this. I'm sorry I was a jerk. I'm sorry I stepped over the line. I'm sorry if I said anything to make you mad. I guess I'm never going to understand the way women think. But from now on, when in doubt I'll err on the side of caution."

"But I *want* you to understand," she insisted quietly. "We've talked about this before. I made a decision about what I think is right for me, and you agreed to respect that decision. So if you care about me, you'll keep your side of the bargain and not try to get me to change my mind when I'm thinking with my body and not with my brain. You'll help me do what I think is best for me. Does that make sense?"

Tom's brows knitted in a frown.

"Would you wave chocolate cake in front of me

if I were trying to lose fifteen pounds?" she teased.

Tom threw back his head and began to laugh. "No," he said. "And I think I catch your meaning, *Ms.* Wakefield." He gave her his most charming smile. "I've just given you a complete and unconditional surrender. Can I put down my hands now?" he asked meekly.

Elizabeth sighed with relief and lifted her arms to hug him. He slid into her embrace and laid his cheek gently on the top of her head.

She smiled into his chest and felt her sense of trust and security begin to return. He was Tom again. Tom, the guy who was her friend. Tom, the guy who was her colleague. Tom, the guy who knew that real men didn't push women to go any further than they wanted to go.

His lips nuzzled her hair and grazed against her ear. "I promise I'll never wave chocolate cake in front of you when you're on a diet," he said softly.

Elizabeth laughed into his shirt, and then socked him in the arm.

Alex restlessly turned again. This was awful. It was the middle of the night, and she was awake. Wide awake. And sober, too.

She'd come back to her dorm room and flopped on the bed with her clothes still on. After a couple of hours' sleep she had awakened—unfortunately sober enough to remember performing some ridiculous dance all by herself in the middle of the Zeta house dance floor.

"Ohhhhhhhh!" she moaned out loud, and covered her face with her hand.

Someone at the party had told her that there was an important meeting at Theta House tomorrow and she needed to be there. Would tomorrow be the day her "sisters" started to make her feel unwelcome?

Tears of humiliation began flowing down her cheeks. What was she going to do? She was self-destructing, and she couldn't seem to stop.

If only she had someone to talk to. But who could she confide in? Not Elizabeth. And not Todd. Todd wasn't her friend. Not really. And he was probably in worse shape than she was.

She turned over, and something crackled and crumpled beneath her cheek. A piece of paper. She removed it from the pillow and stared at it. What was this?

Oh, yeah. That flyer.

FEELING ALL ALONE?
CALL THE CAMPUS HOTLINE FOR A FRIENDLY EAR
24 HOURS A DAY

She looked at the clock. It was late at night. Correction, it was early in the morning. *Oh, for*

86

heaven's sake, she berated herself. *What difference does it make what time it is. It says it's operating twenty-four hours a day.*

"Forget it. I'm not calling any hotline," she snarled at the phone. She dropped the flyer on the floor and turned over again. She was going to sleep. Sleep was the best medicine.

She closed her eyes. But she still saw herself in the bright light of Zeta house. Trying to do some kind of goofy cancan in her tight skirt. Tearing her dress and sending one high-heeled shoe flying into the crowd.

Her finger pressed furiously on her mental clicker. But nothing she did managed to change the channel. She tried station after station, but all she could see was herself, twirling and stumbling into the laughing crowd of Zetas.

Think about something else, she ordered herself. *Think about food, Alex. Or clothes. Or your history paper. Anything.*

But it didn't work. Neither did tossing back and forth. Even banging her head against her pillow didn't help.

"I hate myself!" she finally wailed in frustration.

FEELING ALL ALONE?

"I wish I could just curl up in a little ball and disappear forever!"

"I wish Alexandra Rollins could just fade away, and nobody would even notice or remember."

24 HOURS A DAY

"What a joke!" she wept, reaching for the phone. "Nobody's open twenty-four hours a day."

So why was she calling the place? she wondered as she punched in the number.

Maybe because she had never felt so in despair.

Someone picked up before the first ring had even finished. "Hello?"

The sudden voice caught Alex by surprise and brought her tears to an abrupt halt. "You're really there. You're not a machine!"

"I'm really here," a friendly voice confirmed. "We're here twenty-four hours a day."

"Where's here?" she asked curiously.

"Is that a request for an address or a philosophy question?" He chuckled. The chuckle sounded so warm and reassuring that Alex smiled weakly at her own end of the line. "We're in the student services building," the voice continued.

"That makes sense."

"One of the few things in life that does."

"Now who's talking philosophy," she teased.

There was an appreciative laugh on the other end of the line. Alex held on to the receiver as if it were somebody's hand. "I'm going to guess you didn't call to talk about geography or philosophy. So what *do* you want to talk about?" the voice asked.

Alex opened and closed her mouth a few times.

"Don't know where to start?"

Alex nodded.

"I can't hear you if you nod," the voice reminded her.

She laughed. "Yes. You're right. I don't know where to start."

"If you were talking to a psychologist, he would probably say, *Let's start at the beginning. Tell me about your childhood.* But I'm not a psychologist. I'm just a guy hanging out in the student services building. So why don't we start with tonight. How are you feeling tonight? And what's making you feel that way?"

"I'm feeling humiliated because I went to a party tonight, had too much to drink, and made a complete fool out of myself."

The voice laughed. "You and three-quarters of the Sweet Valley University campus."

That was true. Lots of people at the party had been drunk. Lots of Thetas, too.

"Not that *everybody's doing it* means it's a good thing," he added quickly. "Getting drunk isn't a good thing to do for lots of reasons, and I think you probably know most of them. But my point is this—if you're feeling horrible and miserable because you think every eye was focused on you, then you can probably relax. Most people are too busy thinking about themselves to pay close attention to anybody else."

He was making sense. He was making a lot of sense. She had made a fool of herself, but so had a lot of people. A series of mental pictures flashed before her eyes.

Ryan Frier trying to walk on his hands and falling into a group of girls who definitely did not appreciate his humor.

Samantha Holtzman trying unsuccessfully to whistle through her teeth and spitting on her date's pristine white shirt.

Jeff Cross lying facedown on the floor. Out cold.

"Yeah. You're right," she said slowly. "But I'd still like to stop embarrassing myself on a regular basis. Tonight was supposed to be the beginning of a fresh start. And I blew it."

"You're facing up to the problem. That's a good start toward a fresh start. By the way, you want to tell me your name?"

Alex paused for a long time. She wasn't really sure who she was anymore. Everybody called her Alex, but life as Alex wasn't working out too well. "My name is Enid," she whispered.

"Enid, I've got another line coming in. You

want to hold and we'll talk some more?"

"No. No, I think I can sleep now. Thanks for talking to me. Thanks for listening."

"Believe me, it was my pleasure. Call me anytime you feel like it. Okay?"

"Okay," Enid agreed quietly.

"Good night, then."

"Good night." She started to replace the receiver and then stopped. "Wait!" she shouted into the phone. "Hello. Hello. Are you there?"

"I'm here."

"Who are you? I mean, what's your name? In case I want to call back."

"We're supposed to be an anonymous help line, so we don't use our real names. I'm operator twenty-two. My friends around here call me T Squared because my initials would be *TT*. Did you take enough math to get it?" He chuckled.

"I get it." She laughed. "Good night, T Squared."

"Good night, Enid."

Alex replaced the receiver with a soft click and lay down. For the first time in weeks, she really felt okay. And for the first time in weeks, she knew she was going to sleep peacefully—and not dread the morning.

Elizabeth and Tom disappeared through the double-glass doors that led into Dickenson Hall.

Their light laughter floated back toward William in the cool night air.

He looked at his watch and let out an impatient sigh. He'd been clumsy again. Clumsy and complacent. When Elizabeth had gone to the party with that other girl, he had assumed that she would leave with her, too.

William had counted on them separating at the edge of the quad when they went home. It would be a simple thing to approach Elizabeth in a situation like that. A situation in which she would be alone and forced to listen to him.

Somehow, he had to make her see that none of the unpleasantness she'd suffered at the hands of the secret society had been his idea. She was his goddess. She was the only woman on this campus—probably in the world—who was good enough for him. He had to make her see what a singular honor he was prepared to confer upon her.

But he hadn't figured on that Tom Watts lout meeting her at the party and whisking her away. Watts's car had been right outside Zeta house, and William had no time to get to his own vehicle to pursue them.

He'd had to settle for staking out her dormitory and waiting hours for her return. The window in her room was open, and the light was on.

William could see her standing at the door of her room, telling the boy reporter good night. She closed the door and crossed over to the window. She stood looking out at the night, her face bathed in moonlight.

"Beautiful Elizabeth," he breathed. "If only we could speak. If only we could touch."

BONG BONG BONG BONG

Startled, William jumped as the bell tower began to strike the hour of midnight.

He began to back away, then hurried to the parking lot. He had lingered too long. Now he would have to drive like a demon in order to be back at the Harrington Institution on time.

Thank goodness for Andrea, that pathetically unattractive and ridiculously romantic intern. He had actually convinced her that he was being held as a political prisoner. It had taken only one or two lies and a few passionate kisses to persuade her to give him the keys to her car, the key to the metal grate that covered his window, a magnetic gate pass, and the schedule of room checks.

As William climbed in his car and adjusted the temperature, he checked the clock. He might be a little late for bed check. Damn! Andrea had told him under no circumstances could she lie for him if he wasn't in his room when a doctor came looking.

93

Silly cow! It was a clumsy and transparent way of making sure he returned at night and formed no romantic liaisons with anyone but herself. He laughed out loud. No one told William White what he could or couldn't do. No one. Not Andrea. Not his parents. Not the police.

And as much as he loved her, not Elizabeth Wakefield, either.

Chapter Six

Lila shivered and tried to curl her body even tighter. She wished she and Bruce hadn't argued so much last night. That way they could have slept in each other's arms and been warm. Instead they'd slept yards apart, facing opposite directions. The early-morning sun was streaming down from the sky, but it wasn't hot enough yet to provide any real warmth.

Grrrrr, her stomach growled. Why hadn't Bruce loaded the flare gun? Why? If he had, they could be somewhere warm and comfortable. Somewhere that served good, hot food.

She heard Bruce groan slightly as he began to awaken. Lila turned over and watched him. He was on his back, and she had a clear view of his profile.

His dark tousled hair framed his face, and

there was dark stubble on his cheek. She couldn't help admiring the strong cut of his profile.

Bruce opened his eyes. He must have sensed that he was being watched, because he turned his head to face Lila. They stared into each other's eyes for a moment.

"I'm sorry about the flare gun," he said.

Lila smiled. "Me too."

Bruce sat up and stretched. Lila took in the set of his broad shoulders. They were almost as broad as Tisiano's.

Lila's breath caught in her chest when she realized that for the first time since his death, she hadn't thought about her late husband for the last twenty-four hours.

Was that good or bad? Did it mean she was healing or that her heart was hardening?

Bruce walked over to the cockpit and fished out his pack. "Do we have anything left to eat?" he asked.

Thinking about food made Lila's stomach rumble again. "No," she answered wearily.

He turned his head in her direction and lifted an encouraging eyebrow. "We may have to rely on your Bolivian survival skills. You said something about learning how to set a snare?"

Lila groaned inwardly. Nobody could have

been more amazed than she was when those sticks had actually caught fire yesterday.

True, she had spent eight days in the Bolivian jungle learning survival skills. But she hadn't really applied herself to the task. Mostly she had complained—complained so much that her father had finally threatened to leave her in Bolivia if she didn't stop whining.

Why hadn't she kept her big mouth shut after her success with the fire? Why did she have to go on bragging about being some wilderness expert? Now Bruce was expecting her to rig up something out of twigs and twine to catch them a prairie chicken for breakfast.

"Lila?"

Ever since she could remember, Bruce had loved to give her a hard time about her tendency to show off and exaggerate. If he caught her at it this time, he would really make her life miserable. "I could," she said slowly. "But I don't want to."

"Why not?" he demanded.

She raked her fingers through her matted hair. "I'm just not into killing animals." She shrugged.

He shook his head and rolled his eyes. "You've got to be kidding. I saw you at the Mountain Lodge Inn a few weeks ago, and unless my eyes were deceiving me, that was an eight-ounce salmon steak you were tackling."

"Fish are different," she said.

Bruce's eyebrows began to rise skeptically toward his hairline.

"I don't know why they're different," she said in a defensive tone. "They just are."

His eyes stared straight ahead.

"Bruce! Say something."

"Fish," he whispered. "That's it. I'll go fishing."

"What are you talking about?"

"Yesterday, when I took off on my own, I came across a stream."

"So what? It's not like we have a fishing rod handy."

"As a matter of fact, we do. I saw one in the plane last night—granted, it was in a few pieces."

"Do you know how to fish?"

"Do I know how to fish?" He gave her a broad, confident smile. "While you were trapping in the Bolivian jungle, my dad and I were fishing in Nova Scotia."

"Really?"

Bruce nodded. "Come on. Let's go get breakfast."

Bruce assembled the expensive fishing rod and

attached one of the brightly colored flies to the hook.

Behind him Lila sat on a rock, watching his every move. So far, he looked good. And so far, he was managing to figure everything out.

Bruce nervously bit his lower lip. He was taking a big chance here. The chance that he would look like the world's biggest jerk. He hadn't actually ever fished.

He'd never even set foot in Nova Scotia. But at this point, Bruce figured he had nothing to lose. Lila was making him feel like such an idiot, he had to do something to counteract the bad impression he was making.

His fingers began to tangle in the jumble of wires, and Bruce wished he had paid more attention in Boy Scouts. He was a big guy. And masculine. But in an urban way.

He flipped the rod back and forth experimentally. It was great. The thing whipped back and forth just like in the movies, and the shimmering line flew out over the foamy surface of the choppy water.

"I didn't realize you fished along rapids," Lila said.

Bruce frowned and felt like kicking himself again. How could he be so stupid? He wasn't going to catch anything in this kind of water.

Water that was bubbling and foaming as it swirled around the rocks. "Um, fishing the rapids is for the advanced outdoorsman," he called to her over his shoulder.

Now what? He bit his lip, thinking. What he should probably do was dangle the line for ten minutes or so to make it look good, and then move on to calmer water with a disappointed look on his face.

"You really look like you know what you're doing," Lila said with a note of admiration in her voice.

Bruce acknowledged the compliment with a wink.

"Isn't it dangerous to stand on that rock like that? I mean, what if something pulls you into the water?"

Bruce frowned again. Damn! She was right. He hadn't thought of that. "Hey, give me a break, will you? I won't tell you how to snare possum in the Bolivian jungle if you won't tell me how to fish in the rapids of Nova Scooo*oooohhhh noooo!*

He was falling. Something had jerked hard on his fishing line and pulled him right into the ice-cold water.

"Help!" he shouted. He tried desperately to swim toward the bank, where Lila was leaning down over the water with her hand out-stretched.

"Grab my hand!" she yelled.

Bruce forced his arms to slice against the rushing water. His muscles strained in agony as he swam, hand over hand. But it was no use. Slowly but surely, he was being forced down-stream.

Jessica smoothed her hair and fluffed her bangs with her fingers. She and Isabella stood at the end of the block, ready to go to Theta House. Jessica was glad Isabella had offered to walk in with her. And she knew that whichever way it went, Isabella would always be her friend.

Jessica hoped things would go well. She really wanted to be a Theta pledge again. Wanted to get her life back on track.

Before Mike McAllery had come along and de-railed her academic life, her social life, and her emotional equilibrium, she'd had no trouble fit-ting in and making friends. It would be nice to be that person again. The popular, successful, sought-after freshman pledge.

"Nervous?" Isabella asked.

Jessica shook her head. "No. Yes. I don't know." She had a strange, slightly sick feeling in the pit of her stomach.

"Let's do it," Isabella said, slapping Jessica's hand in a brisk high five.

The two girls hurried down the block and up the steps of Theta House. Jessica gave her bangs one last fluff, and Isabella opened the door and ushered her in.

Jessica caught her breath. It looked like every single Theta was sitting in the living room. Magda sat in a big wing chair, with a straight chair positioned on either side. Alison sat in one, staring malevolently at Jessica.

"Sit down, Jessica." Magda gestured to the last empty chair, and Jessica slowly took her seat.

The air was thick with tension, and there was an expectant hush.

Magda stood and addressed the group. "As you know, we're here today to hold a house vote on whether or not to let Jessica back in as a pledge."

There were a few murmurs, and Magda waited for them to subside before she continued.

"According to Theta rules, since Alison Quinn is the one who wants to blackball Jessica, it's up to her to explain why. When she's finished, we'll vote."

Magda sat and Alison stood. "My case is short and simple. Jessica Wakefield is a liar. She would not be an asset to this sorority, because we can't trust her. If we let her back in as a pledge, eventually she'll become an active. One of our sisters. Nobody wants a sister who can't be trusted."

Jessica felt her face growing white with anger and embarrassment. Her eyes scanned the room, mentally polling the group.

Some girls saw Alison as dedicated to the organization and committed to protecting its interests. Others thought she was just plain mean. Either way, the deck was stacked. The members who believed in Alison would vote with her because they trusted her. The girls who thought she was conniving and power hungry would vote with her because they'd be afraid not to.

"From day one," Alison continued, "Jessica has demonstrated a pattern of dishonesty. She impersonated her sister during rush so that she could trick us into inviting Elizabeth to join. She secretly married Mike McAllery and then lied about it. She had a job that she was ashamed of, so she lied again and told us that she wasn't waiting tables."

Jessica's hands began to shake. Everything Alison had said was true. But the way she was saying it made it all sound so sinister.

"Jessica is a liar, a phony, and a thief. If she really cared about this sorority, she would just bow out. But no. She's going to make us do it the hard way. I think we have to show her, and ourselves, that we play hardball when it comes to honesty issues. That's all I have to say."

Alison sat down with a self-satisfied smirk on her face. Jessica looked around the room. Was there anybody on her side?

Isabella gave her a reassuring smile, but no one else would look her in the eye. Jessica's palms began to sweat. Alison had sounded pretty convincing. "Can I say something?" Jessica asked Magda.

Magda shook her head. "Sorry, Jessica. That's not the way a house vote operates. Technically this is strictly a sorority matter. Since you're not a member or a pledge, it's really not appropriate for you to participate in the discussion."

There was no malice in her voice. But no hint of sympathy either. Jessica knew that Magda took formal sorority proceedings very seriously. Like a judge, she was maintaining a studied and impartial posture.

Magda pressed her lips together. "Everybody form a circle around Jessica, please."

It took the girls a matter of seconds to form a ring around Jessica.

"We'll start with Carol," Magda said, "and work clockwise. When it's your turn to vote, turn your back to vote *out* and stay put if you're voting *in*."

Carol Winthrop was a tall brunette who had always been friendly. But as Jessica watched, her eyes moved back and forth between Jessica's face and Alison's.

Alison Quinn's face was an unforgiving mask, and Jessica saw Carol nervously lick her lips. Would Carol have the nerve to vote against the vice president's wishes?

Carol's eyes briefly met Jessica's, and then fell to the floor. Slowly she turned her back.

Gail Howe, a petite strawberry blonde who had never been very friendly, didn't even pause half a second to deliberate. She turned so fast, she looked like a ballerina executing a crisp pirouette.

One by one, members turned their backs. Jessica blinked hard, fighting the tears.

Alison threw her a cruel smile when the vote reached Jeanne Palmer. The vote had gone halfway around the circle, and every single girl had voted Jessica out. All it would take was one more vote against her, and they would have reached a majority decision. When Jeanne turned her back, Jessica dropped her head in despair.

Chapter Seven

Alex quietly pushed open the front door to Theta House and paused. She heard voices—it sounded like a meeting was in progress.

Very carefully, she closed the door behind her and tiptoed into the front hall.

"I wouldn't be staring at the carpet if I were you," Alex heard a familiar voice sneer. "I'd be taking a good long look around. This is the last time you'll see the inside of this house."

Alex stepped into the living room and froze. Good grief. She'd pictured herself sneaking quietly into the meeting and taking a seat in the back row. She'd had no idea there was some kind of ceremony going on.

"You're late," Magda said with a frown. "This is a house vote. Please find a place in the circle."

Jessica lifted her head, and Alex saw the tears streaming down her cheeks. "What's going on?" Alex asked softly. She could hardly believe she was looking at Jessica Wakefield. Jessica had always been popular, confident, and poised. Now she looked as down and defeated as Alex had felt last night at the Zeta party.

Alison let out an impatient sigh. "Some pledge class we got this year." She nodded toward Jessica. "A bad seed." She nodded at Alex. "And a deadweight."

Alex recoiled as if she had been slapped.

"Alex is totally clueless about what goes on around here," Alison continued in her nastiest voice. "She doesn't show up for events. She doesn't help with any of the work. And she doesn't come to meetings. When she finally decides to grace us with her presence, she looks like she spent the night in a paper bag."

Alex began to feel sick. She'd awakened this morning feeling hopeful and happy after talking with T Squared. The world had seemed a brighter place, and she'd come to Theta House determined to make amends.

Now she felt miserable, guilty, and out of place. Being the target of Alison's go-for-the-throat tirade was like being bludgeoned to death.

"Cool it, Alison," Magda ordered. She turned

her attention to Alex. "We're trying to decide whether or not to let Jessica back in as a pledge. Alison wants to blackball her."

"Blackball Jessica?" Alex repeated softly. "For what?"

"For blowing a simple dare and letting herself get caught by campus security," Alison snapped. "For making us look bad."

Alex stared at Alison. Something about her voice tripped a wire. There was something she needed to remember. Something important.

"What do you mean, she knows you were the tipster? How could she possibly know?"

"Who cares? She knows I turned her in. And she's more or less put two and two together. She's figured out the whole thing was a setup."

The memory of Alison's conversation with Peter Wilbourne came flooding back with so much clarity that it almost knocked Alex off her feet.

She hadn't known what they were talking about last night. But now it was beginning to make sense. Alison had set out to destroy Jessica.

And she knew she could get away with it.

Why?

What made Alison so arrogant? So sure of her power?

" . . . nobody thinks Jessica's word is worth spit these days. She's got no credibility."

That's why.

Peter Wilbourne had been right. Jessica's word wasn't worth much these days. Sure, her prestige had gone up a little since she'd started dating James Montgomery.

But the cloud of intrigue and scandal still hung over her head. Having a bad reputation made her an easy target for somebody like Alison.

Alex pushed her hair back off her brow and massaged her temple.

"Don't stand there gaping," Alison snapped. "Cast your vote and then go sleep it off."

There was a note of disgust in Alison's voice. And a note of *warning*. Warning Alex not to cross her.

Alex and Jessica had never been close friends. Alex didn't owe Jessica anything. If she voted in her favor, she would antagonize Alison.

Right now the vice president just disliked her. But if she willfully thwarted her, she would be Alison's next target. And Alex didn't want Alison Quinn for an enemy.

Magda nodded. "Alison's right. You might as well go ahead and vote," she said.

Jessica's eyes pleaded with her, but Alex looked away. Why should she risk her own skin for Jessica? Jessica had never lifted a finger to help her.

"We're waiting, Alex," Alison reminded her in a bullying tone.

Alex opened her mouth to speak, but she couldn't. Her mind was racing faster and faster, trying desperately to analyze the situation.

If Alison could plot against and then destroy Jessica because she was a "liar," there was no telling what she could do to a girl who was a "drunk."

Alison had to be stopped. Not just for Jessica's sake. Or for Alex's. For the good of the sorority.

"Alex!" Alison barked. "Are you even awake?"

She still didn't know what the *best* thing to do was.

So all she could do was the *right* thing.

Alex lifted her eyes and forced them to meet Alison's hateful stare. "You're the liar," she said quietly. "And I vote Jessica in!"

Elizabeth looked at her watch for the fifth time. She nervously tucked her T-shirt down farther into the waistband of her jeans and tightened the ponytail that hung from the back of her baseball cap.

The Thetas would be holding their house vote right about now. That meant that her sister was feeling either incredibly elated or totally depressed. She wished she hadn't pushed Maia to meet her

110

outside the library so early. They should have met in the twins' room, so that Elizabeth could be there in case Jessica came back a basket case.

There was a low wall in front of the library. Elizabeth went over and sat down where she could look out at the lush campus. Several people were taking advantage of the cool morning and jogging along the track that had been worn around the perimeter of the central quad.

Elizabeth tapped her foot. Maia hadn't been eager to work on this assignment, but she had committed to meet Elizabeth this morning. It wasn't like her to be late. Maybe she had overslept.

Or maybe she was still sick. She had left the Zeta party very suddenly. Maybe Elizabeth should go over to Maia's room and check on her. Or maybe she should go back to her own room and call. That way she could leave a note for Jessica about where to find her if she needed her.

Elizabeth got up and paced back and forth, trying to decide what to do. She chewed the inside of her cheek, thinking about Jessica and the Thetas. She wanted Jessica to be happy. But she couldn't understand why her twin was so eager to be a part of an organization that had treated her so badly.

She started in the direction of her room, then

stopped when she heard Maia's voice. "Hey, you. Where are you going?"

Elizabeth turned. "Maia!"

Maia adjusted her backpack. "Were you giving up on me?"

"No. I was going back to my room to call you. How are you feeling?"

Maia shrugged. "Not so hot."

There were dark circles under her eyes, and her color wasn't very good. "Is it your head or your stomach?" Elizabeth asked.

"Hmm? My head, I guess. Why were you going to your room to call me? That's a long way to go to make a phone call, isn't it?"

"I thought I would check on Jess."

"What's with Jessica?"

Quickly Elizabeth filled her in on what had been going on with the Thetas. "I don't get it," she said finally. "I don't get the way they think. It's like the sorority set the standard of behavior— and then penalized Jess for living up to it."

Maia gave her a wry smile. "Strange. That's exactly the way guys treat girls."

"Meaning?"

"Meaning guys supposedly want girls to be sexy and flirty and sleep with them. And then when a girl behaves that way, they turn around and act like she's a slut or something."

Elizabeth readjusted her baseball cap so that the bill blocked the sun. "That's an interesting observation. Maybe we should make that our editorial topic."

Maia's face immediately closed a little. "Maybe," she agreed. There was a definite lack of enthusiasm in her voice.

It was all Elizabeth could do not to let her frustration show. What was it with Maia? Every time Elizabeth brought up the assignment, she shut down or got cranky. She shot down every idea either by outright veto —or displaying no interest whatsoever.

"So do you want to go back to your room or what?" Maia asked after a short silence.

Elizabeth was torn. If she went back to her room and Jessica *did* come in upset, Maia might leave and Elizabeth would never pin her down on getting together again. "No. Let's get to work. The sooner we get finished, the sooner we can enjoy a little of this gorgeous day."

Maia nodded, and the two girls made their way into the library. There weren't many people around. Jack Baker, a friend of Elizabeth's, was manning the front desk. A stack of books stood at his elbow, and he quickly and efficiently opened the back cover of each and scanned the card with a computerized pen.

He looked up and grinned when he saw Elizabeth.

She grinned back. "Any chance you might give us a key to one of the graduate carrels?"

The graduate carrels were little rooms in the basement with doors that closed. They were very private and great for collaborative assignments because you could talk naturally and not have to whisper.

Elizabeth gave him a dazzling smile. Jack gulped and pretended to stamp his hand by mistake. Elizabeth and Maia laughed as he fished under the desk for the keys. "For you, Liz, anything," Jack answered. He handed her a key on a large fuzzy pair of dice. "But if a grad student asks for the carrel, you guys have to clear out, okay?"

"No problem." Elizabeth took the key and smiled her thanks. "Come on, Maia. We're in basement carrel *D*, behind the stacks."

More students drifted into the lobby behind them as they entered the main part of the library and headed for the rear. Elizabeth glanced left and right. The building was quiet. Very quiet.

Elizabeth felt a familiar sense of unease as they descended the stairs and walked past the old stacks of out-of-print and rare books. The hairs on the back of her neck stood up, and she had the oddest feeling that she was being watched.

A sudden movement to her left caught her attention, and she came to an abrupt halt. A hunched-over figure in a wheelchair zipped across an aisle several yards away and disappeared behind a large bookshelf.

"Elizabeth?" Maia whispered, standing at the door of carrel *D*. "Are you coming?"

"Yeah. It's just—"

"What?"

"That guy in the wheelchair. He gives me the creeps. Whenever I'm around, he's lurking in the shadows."

"And I thought I was getting paranoid," Maia said with a short laugh.

Elizabeth hurried to the door and unlocked it. Once inside, she closed the door, removed her baseball cap, and sat down at small worktable with three chairs gathered around it. "So," she chirped in a cheerful voice. "How do you want to start?"

Maia gave her a stony stare and let out an aggravated sigh. "People talk about gender issues and argue about them and write about them, but nothing ever changes. This assignment is such a joke."

Irritation and impatience got the better of Elizabeth, and she snapped. "Look, Maia, all I know is that Tuesday afternoon you and I have to turn in a fifteen-hundred-word editorial on a gender issue, and that's *no joke*. Now, I don't know what the big problem is here, but if you don't want to work on it, that's fine. Just get out of my way and let me write it. Because I don't plan on taking an *F* for this assignment."

"I didn't say I wasn't going to do the assignment," Maia retorted.

"Then quit biting my head off every time I bring up an idea."

"I can't help it. Some of your ideas about this stuff are silly."

"Silly?" Elizabeth blinked in surprise. She couldn't believe Maia was being so insulting. "Yesterday I was just naive. Today I'm silly. Excuse me, Maia, but would you please tell me what makes you the expert on gender issues?"

"Forget it," Maia grumbled, removing her notebook from her backpack.

"No. Let's not forget it."

"I'm sorry," Maia said. "Please, let's forget it, okay?" Her face looked so truly distressed and unwell that Elizabeth forgot her anger. Instinctively she stretched her hand across the table to take Maia's. "Is your head really that bad? Do you want a couple of aspirin? Jack keeps some behind the desk."

Maia laughed bitterly. "I don't have a headache. When I said the problem is my head, I guess I should have said the problem was with my brain. I can't sleep anymore. I have so many bad dreams, I'm afraid to close my eyes at night." She pulled the voluminous windbreaker she wore closer around her.

"What do you dream about?" Elizabeth asked.

Maia shrugged. "I don't know." Her fingers twitched at the collar of her jacket.

"I think you do," Elizabeth said softly. "It might help if you talked about it. If not to me, then to somebody else."

"No," Maia whispered. "There's nobody I want to talk to about it." Maia's eyes wandered. She looked up. She looked down. She looked at the table. She looked everywhere but at Elizabeth.

Elizabeth was at a complete and utter loss. She'd always been a careful listener. And most of her friends regarded her as a good adviser. But she couldn't seem to reach Maia. Couldn't seem to get to that level of trust. "Maybe you should go for some counseling," she suggested softly. "Student services provides free—"

"Forget it!" Maia's response was so sudden, and so fierce, it was as if Elizabeth had slapped her in the face. "They would want me to name names, and then the administration would get involved. The next thing I know, some dean would be telling me it was my fault. And he'd be right. It was my fault. I was stupid, and now the only thing I can do is let it go and forget about it."

"Forget about *what*? Maia! *What* was your fault?"

Maia's lips trembled, and she wiped the corner of her eye with a shaking finger.

Elizabeth held her breath, afraid that one wrong move, one wrong word would drive Maia out of the room. Maia's head dropped, and her shoulders began to shake. Elizabeth said nothing, but she moved across the table and sat quietly in the seat beside Maia.

Slowly Maia leaned over until her head was on Elizabeth's shoulder. A shuddering sob racked her shoulders. "I was raped," she choked. "I went out with this guy a few weeks ago and . . . he raped me."

Elizabeth's heart thudded down into her shoes. Of course. How could she not have seen it? The withdrawal. The baggy clothes. The defensive attitude about sexual matters.

No wonder Maia was so unhappy. Rape was the biggest gender issue of them all, and Maia was trying to deal with it all by herself.

Lila raced along the bank, leaping over logs and dodging obstacles in a desperate effort to keep pace with Bruce.

The farther downstream he went, the faster the

water raced. She saw him alternately swimming and bobbing as he tried to navigate the treacherous waters.

She let out a shriek of pain when her foot snagged on a tree root, and she tripped face forward. Something sharp grazed her face, and a lot of her weight fell on her sore elbow.

She struggled to her feet and anxiously scanned the surface of the stream.

He was gone.

"Bruce!" she screamed. "Bruce, where are you?"

Something dark bobbed up out of the water. It was Bruce's head. The head was followed by a red arm that smacked the surface.

Lila began running again, trying to watch the ground and at the same time keep an eye on Bruce as he disappeared again and again beneath the foam. Within seconds, her chest felt as if it were going to burst. She had been running for hours, it seemed, sobbing with fatigue and gasping for breath.

But she couldn't stop. Not as long as there was a chance of saving Bruce. Up ahead, she saw some rocks protruding out of the water. Vines from an overhanging tree fell down over them, creating a shaded nook.

Lila's heart skipped a beat. If Bruce positioned himself correctly and she moved quickly enough, he might have a chance.

She lowered her head and increased her speed. The threat of death seemed to be transforming her from a woman into a gazelle. She leaped over another nest of roots, leaped again onto the nearest rock face, and with an agility that came from desperation, she hurried to the tip of an outcropping. At last she was able to grab a low-hanging vine with one hand. She leaned down, stretching her other hand toward the water. "Grab my hand!" she yelled.

Bruce lifted his arm as he came careening past the outcropping. His hand grasped hers, and the sudden jerk almost pulled Lila into the water. But her other hand gripped the vine so hard, she felt her nails dig into her palm.

Gasping and groaning, Bruce began to pull himself up by using Lila's arm to gain leverage. As he climbed out, his feet skittered against the slippery surface of the rock.

"No!" The jerk when he fell back into the water practically pulled Lila's arm out of her shoulder socket. But she didn't let go, and neither did Bruce. His hand clutched hers so tightly, she could feel the small bones of her hand bending.

He was climbing again now. Carefully searching out toeholds so he wouldn't slip again. Every second seemed like an hour. But finally, miraculously, he was safely out of the water.

"Oh, God! Oh, God!" he panted. His legs seemed to turn to rubber, and he flopped down on the flat warm surface of the rock, gasping like a fish. "I'm alive. I'm alive. I can't believe I'm alive."

Now that the crisis was over, Lila's adrenaline level began to drop. Bruce had had a close call. A very close call. Her own knees began to wobble, and she sank down beside him. "I can't believe you're alive either." She reached for his hand. "You're alive. I'm alive. It must mean something. Don't you think?" His wet shirt clung to his powerful shoulders and chest muscles. Lila's already racing heart began racing even faster.

But Bruce was too busy coughing to answer. With a fatigued groan, he rolled over on his back. "Remind me not to fake any more outdoor skills, will you? It's too dangerous. You win. You're the survival expert. I give up. No contest."

Lila's heart began to thump in an entirely different rhythm. "*Fake* outdoor skills," she repeated incredulously. "You mean like . . . *fishing*?"

Bruce's head moved up and down. "Yeah," he wheezed. "Like fishing."

"You *don't know how to fish*?"

"Never been fishing in my life," he admitted blithely. Bruce clasped his hands behind his neck and closed his eyes, oblivious to Lila's reaction. He lifted his head with his hands and stretched the neck muscle. "Ouch! I think I pulled something." He groaned again and turned over on his stomach. "Lila"—he wriggled his left shoulder blade— "rub my shoulder right *there*, would you?"

A sheen of red rage descended over Lila's vision, and she rose to her feet. "I'll rub you right *there*," she said through gritted teeth. And with that, she kicked him as hard as she could.

"Hey!" Bruce sprang to his feet with a startled cry. "What was that for?"

"For acting like a show-off and pretending you knew how to fish."

She kicked him again—in the right shin. "That was for falling into the water and making me run for two miles. And *this*"—she hoisted her foot and aimed for the other shin—"is for being a prize jerk!"

Bruce managed to sidestep the toe when her knee sprang, but she caught him in the calf with the recoil. He let out a cry of pain. "Cut it out, Lila. I almost drowned. This is not a good time to yell at me." Dripping wet and looking annoyed, he brushed past her and began trudging upstream.

"Where are you going?" she shouted.

"Back to the plane."

"Don't bother to thank me for saving your

life," she said bitterly, scrambling over the rocks and hurrying to catch up with him.

"I won't," he retorted. "Because if I have to spend much more time with you, my life won't be worth living. Now would you just shut up and start figuring out how to snare something for breakfast?"

"I told you," she insisted. "I don't like to kill things."

"No problem. If you'll catch it, *I'll* kill it. And if you can't bring yourself to eat it, that's great. It just means more for me."

Lila stopped and put her hands on her hips, watching him walk angrily through the trees. Now what was she going to do?

"Come on!" he shouted impatiently. "I'm starving."

"That's it?" Magda asked. She stood with her arms across her chest, staring hard at Alex. They were alone in a quiet room, away from the chaos of the meeting. "That's all you heard?"

"That's everything I heard," Alex said with quiet dignity. "Alison's right. I'd had a lot to drink, but I know what I saw and heard."

Magda frowned and looked deep into Alex's eyes. Then she strode to the door of the den off the living room and opened the sliding door.

The loud babble of excited and indignant voices exacerbated Alex's pounding headache. Magda waded out into the crowd and beckoned for Alex to follow her. "Quiet!" she shouted. "Quiet, please."

The roomful of girls buzzed like a beehive. Arguments, speculations, agreements, and accusations flew in every direction.

"Quiet, *please*!" Magda shouted again.

The noise subsided to a dull roar, and Alex caught a glimpse of Alison standing in a corner, surrounded by her core group of friends and henchwomen.

On the other side of the room Jessica sat on a sofa with Isabella and Denise. Her face was white and shaken. But no whiter and shaken than Alex's. Walking in late to a house vote and leveling a damaging accusation at the vice president was a fairly serious breach of Theta courtesy. When Magda had called a halt to the proceedings and taken Alex into the den for a private talk, Alex had been prepared for the worst.

She had no idea what Magda was thinking now. No idea what was going to happen to Jessica. And no idea what was going to happen to her.

Alison broke away from her group and took a step toward Alex. "I think Alex owes me and everybody else an apology. I hope you told her that."

The room began to buzz again, and Magda held up her hand for silence. "I think I'll let Alex tell you what she told me, and then we'll talk about apologies. Alex?"

Alex's heart began to thunder against her ribs. Was Magda backing her up or throwing her to the wolves? She tried to search Magda's expressionless face for some clue.

Alex swallowed. "I overheard Alison and Peter Wilbourne talking last night at the Zeta party," she said in a trembling voice. "It was clear from the conversation that Alison set Jessica up. Then she tipped off campus security to make sure Jessica got caught. I didn't hear a rumor. I didn't hear a secondhand account. I heard the words from her own lips."

She forced herself to look at Alison. Some of the color left Alison's face, but she didn't back down. Her lip lifted in an ugly sneer. "Oh, come on," she said in a voice of disbelief. "You don't *believe* this, do you? Consider the source. Alex probably doesn't know *what* she heard last night. I'm surprised she can even remember where she was."

That was it. Alex had had enough. She'd done what she could for Jessica, but she wasn't going to stand here any longer and be abused by the dragon lady. If they wanted to throw her out, that was fine. She took a step in the direction of the door, but Magda's hand shot out and took hers, pulling her back. "Wait."

"Does Alex have any proof?" someone asked from the back of the room.

"Right. Did anybody else hear the conversation?" Kimberly Schyler wanted to know. "Was anybody with you?"

Alison lifted her brows. "Yes, Alex," she asked in a withering voice of sarcasm. "Do you have any proof? You know it's very irresponsible to make accusations that you can't prove."

"No," Alex said softly. "I don't have any proof."

Alison smiled and dusted her hands together in a dismissive gesture. "Then we're back where we started. My word against Jessica's." She glared at Alex. "And *she* owes me an apology."

"I could call an all-Greek hearing and subpoena Peter," Magda added quietly.

The smug smile left Alison's face, and there were several audible gasps, including one from Alex. She studied Magda's face again. It was clear now that the Theta president believed her. Why?

Alison's pointed chin quivered slightly and her small eyes darted around the room, as if gauging the level of her support.

Because if Magda's president and Alison's vice

president, Alex thought, *she probably knows Alison for what she is. And she knows that if Alison got the chance, she'd be president. Magda's probably been the target of one or two Alison Quinn plots herself.*

Alison drew herself up and lifted her chin. "Do you really think an all-Greek hearing is necessary?" she asked coldly.

"It is if you want an apology, Alison." Magda's voice was pleasant and nonjudgmental, but it was firm. "What do you want to do?"

Alison's face was crumbling, but she said nothing.

There was a long, awkward silence in the room. Several girls stared determinedly at their feet.

When it became apparent that Alison wasn't going to answer the question, Magda spoke. "I think we should get on with the vote," she said quietly. "Let's form the circle again, please."

The girls complied in silence. When the circle was formed, Jessica walked between Alex and Magda to take her place in the center.

As she brushed past Alex, her hand squeezed Alex's upper arm. "Thank you." It was a barely audible whisper, but Alex heard it and was gratified.

"Who had the next vote?" Courtney asked.

"Magda," Gloria Abel answered.

All eyes turned in her direction.

"Magda?" Isabella prompted.

Alex's breath caught in her chest, and it felt as if her heart had ceased to beat.

Magda looked around the room at each and every girl. Then her gaze shifted to Jessica. "In," she said in a firm voice.

Alex let out a long sigh of relief, and her heart resumed its normal rhythm.

Tina Chai stood next to Magda. Her face looked startled for a moment, but then she too stared fixedly ahead. "In," she said.

Girl after girl cast her vote until the circle had been completed. When the vote was over, half the circle was facing away from Jessica, and the other half was facing in.

A little smile flickered across Magda's face. "If anyone would like to change her vote, now's the time to do it."

In less than four seconds almost every girl had turned, facing into the circle now instead of out. The only back still turned toward Jessica was Alison Quinn's.

"The house vote is complete," Magda said. "Jessica, congratulations. You are hereby declared a Theta pledge." The silence was broken by a loud round of applause. Isabella and Denise hurried forward and hugged Jessica. The configuration of the circle began to disappear as several of the girls rushed to congratulate her.

"Please keep your places," Magda requested. "I'd like to say something."

The girls fell back into place.

"Sororities are about sisterhood," Magda continued. "Or they're supposed to be, anyway. If all we've done here today is create a big rift, we haven't solved any problems."

"What are you saying?" Pam Stanger asked.

"I'm saying that if Jessica and Alison can't be sisters, then Alison is going to have to go. And I think in all fairness, the decision should be Jessica's."

Jessica's face registered shock. Alex's own eyes widened in surprise. A *pledge* was going to be given blackball power over an *active*?

Alex couldn't believe it. It was incredible. It was beautiful. Talk about poetic justice. Maybe the Thetas had more integrity than she'd been giving them credit for.

Every eye turned in Jessica's direction.

"Well, Jessica," Isabella said in a soft voice. "What's it going to be?"

"I'd like to think it over," Jessica announced.

Chapter Eight

"What do you mean, you don't know how to track or snare?" Bruce yelled. "I thought you studied survival in the jungle!"

Lila pressed her lips together. She'd hoped it wouldn't come to this. She had led Bruce around the woods for almost an hour in the hope that she might actually spot something edible. But the only things they had spotted were birds and one or two squirrels. Unfortunately all the wildlife was staying safe and sound in the trees.

Finally she had been forced to admit that she didn't have the slightest idea what she was doing.

Bruce eyed her shins longingly. "Don't even think about it," she warned.

Bruce kicked at a pinecone in frustration, then sat down on a fallen log. He shook his head and dropped it into his hands. "I'm going to die!"

Lila sat down on the log next to him. "So am I, but you don't hear me sniveling."

"No, you're not going to die," he said quietly. "At least I hope not. But I think I am." There was something strangely calm about his voice. Straightforward and matter-of-fact and completely devoid of melodrama. It wasn't like Bruce, and Lila began to feel uneasy.

"How come you're going to die and I'm not?" she demanded.

Bruce reached over, took her hand, and pressed it to his forehead.

She gasped. "You've got a fever. You're burning up! When did that start?"

"This morning. I woke up with it."

"Why didn't you say anything?"

"I didn't think I was this sick."

"You probably weren't. But that water was freezing. Bruce! You probably made whatever's wrong fifty times worse." She was close to panicking. If this turned into pneumonia, he could be dead in a matter of hours. "Let's go back to the plane," she said in a husky voice. "I'll try to start another fire. We've got to get you warm."

Elizabeth turned the page and forced her eyes to scan the columns of tiny print in her history textbook. She had twenty pages of reading to get through tonight. She took a deep breath, then exhaled and turned the page back again.

Who was she kidding? She hadn't absorbed anything. Her mind absolutely, positively refused to cooperate tonight. There were just too many other things to think about.

Jessica, for one. Elizabeth glanced at the clock. She had been waiting all afternoon to hear from Jessica, and the suspense was killing her. She wished her sister would at least call so Elizabeth could stop worrying that she was hiding somewhere sobbing her eyes out.

Her chair creaked as she tipped back in it and stared at the wall. That conversation with Maia had left her oddly disoriented. Date rape in the abstract was one thing. When it happened to someone you knew, it was something different altogether. It was personal. Immediate. Like being violated yourself.

"It could have been me," she muttered to herself.

Or could it?

The incident with Tom replayed itself in her head. She hadn't hesitated to shout when she had to. But that was because she knew Tom. She knew that no matter what, he would never hurt her.

But what if she hadn't been with Tom? What if she had been with someone else? Someone whose temper she didn't trust? A picture of William White flitted through her thoughts. She might have been afraid to shout. Afraid to resist.

Hmmm. Could she get fifteen hundred words out of that? She sat forward and reached for the keypad of her computer. The nature of the assignment was too emotionally charged for Maia.

If Maia didn't want to go to counseling and didn't want to report the incident to the authorities, then there wasn't a lot that Elizabeth could do to help her. But she could finish the journalism assignment on her own and spare Maia the discomfort of having to write about something so painful.

Elizabeth's fingers moved efficiently over the keypad. It was a hard subject to write about. But challenging. And important. The time passed quickly, and before she knew it, the piece was almost done.

She was pleased with the way it was turning out. Maybe she'd send it to the newspaper for the op-ed page.

The door flew open with a bang, and Elizabeth jumped as Jessica flung herself into the room with her fist raised in a victory salute. "If only you had been there," Jessica breathed, her blue-green eyes bright with excitement. "It was great, Lizzie. It was just like in the movies."

"I take it you're back in."

"Thanks to . . . guess who?"

"Me!"

"Thanks to Enid, a.k.a. Alex," Jessica corrected.

"You're kidding! What happened?"

"Has Lila called?"

Elizabeth shook her head. "Nobody called."

Jessica frowned. "Wow! It's not like her to stay out of touch for so long. Oh, well, I'll have to tell her about it later." She hurried over and sat down at the foot of Elizabeth's bed. "It turns out that Alex overheard Alison Quinn telling Peter Wilbourne all about her plot at the Zeta party last night."

"Did she have a tape recorder with her?"

"Nope. But Magda believed her—and so did everybody else."

"Why?"

"I guess because setting me up like that is exactly the kind of thing Alison *would* do. It boiled down to . . . what do you call it?"

"Credibility?"

"Right. Credibility. The upshot is that Alex and I have credibility, and Alison Quinn has squat."

"So did she slink out of the house snarling *Curses, foiled again*? Or did everybody have a cup of tea and shake hands?"

134

"Neither. *I* get to decide whether Alison stays in or gets kicked out." Her face darkened. "And for the fifteenth time, I wish you wouldn't be so sarcastic about the Thetas. It makes it impossible to talk to you about anything, and . . ."

"Sorry! Sorry!" Elizabeth said quickly, hoping to stem the flow. She wasn't in the mood for a The Thetas Are Really Great Girls speech. "I'm through being sarcastic," she promised. "And I'm really, really glad you got what you wanted."

The phone rang, and Jessica dove toward it. "Maybe that's Lila." She lifted the receiver to her ear with a broad smile on her face. "Hello?"

Her face fell a fraction, and she handed it to Elizabeth. "For you. It's Tom."

Elizabeth smiled and cradled the receiver against her shoulder. "Hi."

"Do you ever go out on school nights?"

"I might be persuaded. What did you have in mind?"

"There's a Humphrey Bogart double feature at the University Bijou. It starts in half an hour. Can you make it?"

Elizabeth expelled her breath with a loud sigh. Reading tonight was probably out of the question. But there were a lot of notes she needed to type. And a bunch of notebooks to clean out.

But cleaning the cobwebs out of her brain was

important too. Elizabeth leaned forward and tapped "save" on the keypad. "I can make it."

"I'll pick you up in front of your dorm in ten minutes," he said.

Elizabeth hung up the phone and went over to the mirror that hung over her bureau. "I'm going out with Tom. There's a double feature at the Bijou."

"The Humphrey Bogart festival, right? I saw James on the way back to the dorm and he asked me to go." Jessica hopped up and opened the closet door, gazing at the contents with a speculative gleam in her eye. "Now, let's see." She pulled out a navy blue sweater dress and held it up. "What do you think?'

Elizabeth grinned. "It's a little conservative. But it's got credibility written all over it."

"Shhho, shhweetheart," Tom slurred, mimicking Humphrey Bogart, "what's it gonna be? Pizza or a burger?"

"Hmmm?"

Tom took her arm and pulled her gently to a stop. "You know, that's about the tenth time you've gone 'hmmmm?' since I picked you up. Have you got something on your mind besides me?"

Elizabeth smiled. Tom was disturbingly percep-

tive sometimes. The noise in the large, old-fash-
ioned lobby got louder and louder as people
surged out of the theater. She lifted her hand in a
wave at Nina Harper and Bryan Nelson on the
other side of the lobby just before they left
through the side exit. "Let's get a burger," she
said.

Tom wove his arm through hers, and they left
the theater and strolled slowly down the street
past the card shop, the bath shop, the bookstore,
and the Chinese restaurant.

Two minutes later they were seated in a back
booth at Harry's Burgers, waiting for two
Harryburger specials—hamburgers served with
everything imaginable.

"Quick movie review, and then we'll talk about
what's on your mind," Tom said. "First feature . . ."
He turned his thumb down. "Second feature . . ."
He turned his thumb up.

Elizabeth shook out her blond hair and gave
him an apologetic smile. "I'm sorry. I guess I
wasn't paying enough attention to have an
opinion."

Tom sat back and let his lower jaw hang agape.
"Wow! Whatever's on your mind must be big stuff
if it can block out Humphrey Bogart."

He looked so happy, so handsome, and so
pleased to be out with her that Elizabeth almost

137

hated to bring up the topic of what had happened to Maia. "Tom," she began. "I need to tell you something that happened to a friend of mine."

"Something bad?"

"Bad would be the understatement of the year."

They both fell silent as the waitress appeared at their table, dropped two plates loaded with burgers and fries, and then hurried off.

When she was out of earshot, Elizabeth leaned forward and spoke in a low tone. In as few words as possible, and as unemotionally as possible, she recounted what Maia had told her.

"Wow!" Tom took a bite of his hamburger and chewed thoughtfully. He swallowed, took a sip of his soda, and then wiped his mouth. "This happened to somebody you know?"

Elizabeth nodded.

Tom didn't actually push away his plate, but Elizabeth could sense his loss of appetite from the way he sat slightly back in the booth and away from his plate. He looked at Elizabeth and pressed his lips together. "Are you telling me this because of what happened last night? Because I thought we'd covered that and moved on. But if you're still mad—"

"This isn't about us," Elizabeth said, cutting him off. "Not about you, anyway. Because you're not the kind of guy who would ever do something like that. But it's about me, because it could have been me—don't you realize that?"

Tom smiled wryly. "No, it couldn't, Elizabeth. You're very clear about what you do and do not want to do. You're not the kind of girl who . . ." Tom bit his lip, as if he were trying to pick his words very carefully.

"Who what?"

Tom shifted uncomfortably.

"Who what?" Elizabeth pressed.

"Who sends mixed signals."

Elizabeth frowned. "I thought we already discussed this. I thought you understood. How many times do women have to say it? No means no, and—"

"Yeah, well, sometimes girls don't say no," he interrupted in an angry voice.

"What?"

"Sometimes girls don't say no," he repeated, his eyelashes fluttering. "I agree with you. No means no, but sometimes . . ." He rocked back and forth. "Sometimes girls don't say no," he repeated in a defensive tone.

Her mouth opened in surprise. Was he serious?

"Sometimes girls don't say no until the next morning. It happens, Elizabeth. Sometimes girls say yes and then, if they wind up disappointed or get their feelings hurt, they decide they meant no.

It's a hell of a way to get even with a guy."

"Oh, man," Elizabeth breathed, putting her hand to forehead. "That's not what happened."

"Well, you see, Liz," Tom continued in the same defensive tone, "here's the problem. You don't really know what happened, and neither do I."

"I know my friend."

"Sex makes people do strange things," he said shortly. "As you found out last night—and for which I *once again* apologize."

Suddenly Elizabeth was furious. Furious and upset. "Why are you being so horrible about this?" she asked, her voice breaking. "It makes me feel a million miles away from you."

"I was on the football team. It gets old having girls lecture you all the time because you're an athlete. Always acting like you're some horrible predator. A potential rapist." Tom's hands gripped the edge of the table, and Elizabeth could see his knuckles turning white. "It's insulting."

Elizabeth took some deep breaths, struggling hard to keep her voice from sounding accusatory and emotional. "I agree. And I don't blame you for being angry. But your anger is totally misdirected."

"Huh?"

"You're angry at girls who think you're a rapist because you're an athlete. You should be angry at the athletes who think wearing a jersey is a license to rape. *They're* the ones who give players a bad reputation—not the girls who report them." Elizabeth bit her lower lip to keep from crying. She felt miserable and sick to her stomach.

Tom fidgeted with his fork, his eyes flickering around the room while his jaw muscles worked.

Elizabeth dropped her eyes and stared down into her lap. Did Tom really not understand? Were all men, no matter how decent and kind and caring, at heart so callous that they simply refused to condemn guys who stepped out of line? If so . . . Elizabeth could hardly bear to finish the thought. But she sure couldn't put much trust in a man who thought like that.

After what seemed like an hour, she heard him let out his breath in a long, loud sigh. "Elizabeth," he said.

She lifted her eyes and saw him staring levelly across the table. He dropped the fork with a clatter and ran his hand over the top of his head in a gesture of bemusement. "You're right," he said, the muscles of his face beginning to relax. "You're absolutely right. What do you want me to do?"

"Stop blaming the victim," she blurted. "You're a part of the media, and so am I. What we have to do is be more sensitive in the way we handle reporting. Stop reporting what the victim was or wasn't wearing. Whether she had or had not been drinking. Don't put the victim on trial. And stop looking the other way when other guys act like jerks. Make it clear that you don't think that mistreating women is funny or manly or acceptable. Then maybe girls like my friend wouldn't be afraid to speak up."

"And maybe we wouldn't have a rapist walking around loose on our campus," Tom added. He slouched his back and lifted his head. "Do you have any idea who it was?"

Elizabeth shook her head. "None." She was still upset, and her mouth was trembling.

Tom leaned forward and took her hand. "Hey," he said softly. "Everything you say makes perfect sense to me. I'm not your enemy. I'm not any girl's enemy. But I'm still learning, okay? I'm learning as fast as I can, but I can't know what it's like to walk around in your body and see the world through your eyes. Sometimes I have to wait for you to tell me."

"I'm telling you now," Elizabeth said thickly.

He leaned over the table and kissed her on the forehead. "And I'm listening. I'm listening to every word."

Alex pulled a brush through her auburn hair and studied her face. It hadn't been quite twenty-four hours since she'd had a drink, but she looked better already. Her eyes didn't have that slightly red tinge. And her cheeks didn't have that weird flush.

The brush felt good against her scalp. It made all the thousands of little muscles in her forehead and the back of her neck relax.

It had been some day, and she was still wound up from head to toe. "I'll never sleep tonight," Alex muttered to her reflection. "Never. My nervous system is on overload."

The scene at Theta House this morning had really blown her away. Walking into the house vote like that had been a nightmare. All those girls looking at her like she was a freak. She shivered. "Yuck!"

Then having that private talk with Magda! That was even worse. Alex had always been a little afraid of Magda. And a little envious. She seemed so poised. So in control of herself and everything that happened around her.

Alex didn't feel in control of anything. And when she drank, she was even more out of control. Coming out on top today had made her feel slightly better about things.

Maybe she was being premature, but she felt like this fresh-start business wasn't so impossible after all.

There was a soft knock at the door.

"Who is it?"

"It's me, Todd."

When she opened the door, he gave her a smile. His thick brown hair was combed. His jeans were freshly laundered. And his crisp, oxford cloth shirt was neatly pressed. "Can I come in?" he asked.

"Sure. What's up?" Alex stepped back a bit to let him pass and smelled the liquor on his breath as he brushed by her and walked into the room. *Uh-oh. He looks fine, but he's been drinking*, she thought. *Not enough to get drunk, but just enough to make him come over here.*

Todd shrugged. "I was just feeling a little blue, and I thought I'd stop by and see if you wanted to go out for a drink or something."

At this time yesterday, Alex would have jumped at the invitation. Especially when the alternative was spending the evening alone in her room with nothing but painful memories to keep her company. But not tonight. "I think I'll pass," she answered. "But thanks."

Todd blinked. "No?"

Alex shook her head. "No. I've got an early class tomorrow, and I don't want to be out late."

"So we'll have one drink and split." He smiled. "Better bring a jacket. It's getting cold out there."

"Todd . . ." Alex began. "I don't want to go out for a drink. You and I both know that one drink usually leads to two drinks, and the next thing we know, we're wasted and . . ." She broke off, embarrassed. She didn't know how to say she didn't want to wake up in the morning with only a hazy idea of what had happened the night before.

Todd flushed, and his eyes dropped to the ground. Disappointment was written all over his face.

"It's not that I don't like you, Todd. But I don't know you. Not really."

"You've known me all through high school," he protested. "Whatever there is to know, you know." He let out a rueful laugh. "I'm not that complicated."

"I've known you as Elizabeth's boyfriend. I've known you as the basketball hero of Sweet Valley High. I've known you as class president. But now—" She shook her head in confusion.

"And now I'm Todd Wilkins, big nothing," he said coldly. "I'm not Elizabeth Wakefield's boyfriend. I'm not the class president." He laughed bitterly. "And believe me, I'm painfully aware that I'm no kind of hero—basketball or otherwise. So now that I'm down here on the ground with all the other mere mortals, even Enid Rollins doesn't want to be seen with me."

145

Even Enid Rollins. The remark stung, and her palm itched to slap him back.

All her life she had been *poor* Enid Rollins or *little* Enid Rollins. And during her druggie phase in high school, she'd been *that* Enid Rollins. College had given her an opportunity to reinvent herself completely. She hadn't done too great a job. But that didn't mean she was going to stand here in her own room and let Todd put her down.

Even Enid Rollins, he'd said in a voice of disbelief. Like she was so far below him she should have been grateful he was willing to give her the time of day.

"You're right," she said coldly. "I don't want to be seen with you. I don't want to be seen with any guy who puts me down."

Todd's eyes widened with surprise, and he took a wary step back. Obviously he wasn't used to Alex standing up for herself.

For that matter, *Alex* wasn't used to standing up for herself. And she wasn't quite sure how to handle it. All she knew was that Todd owed her an apology. And if she didn't get it—that was it for their friendship, or buddyship, or reboundship— or whatever it was they had between them.

Todd met her level stare, and then his lips disappeared. He hung his head slightly. "I'm sorry, Alex. I'm really, really sorry. I get so busy feeling bad about my own life that I forget other people have feelings. That was a lousy thing to say."

Suddenly Alex felt sorry for him. He looked depressed. Depleted. Like a guy who had lost everything that ever meant anything to him.

And he had, she reflected. He'd lost Elizabeth. He'd lost his spot on the basketball team. He'd lost his scholarship. He'd lost the respect of his classmates and friends.

He was down to ground zero. Right next to Alex.

But Alex was ready to start over, and she couldn't do it hanging on to Todd. "Todd. I need to clean up my act, and so do you," she said bluntly. "If you want to know the truth, I don't think we're very good for each other."

His face looked pale and sick. His forehead and cheeks were covered with a sheen of perspiration. His voice broke. "I don't have a whole lot of friends left." He took her hand, and his eyes searched her face. "Please be my friend. Please," he added softly. "You're down in the dumps too, that's all. Probably had a bad day. Let's go have a drink and we'll talk about it some more. Okay?"

He put his hand on her cheek and leaned forward to kiss her, but she jerked her head away. "No."

Todd reared back, his face a mixture of hurt and anger. "Alex!"

"It's late," she said in a flat voice.

Todd turned wearily. "Yeah. Okay," he breathed. "I'll see you around."

"Good night," she said as he let himself out.

Todd didn't answer, and the door slammed shut behind him.

Alex sat on the bed, her heart beating fast. She didn't like hurting Todd, and she wasn't comfortable having him be angry with her. But she didn't know how else to make him take her seriously.

She realized her hands were shaking, and she felt like she was going to burst into hysterical tears. Why had Todd come over tonight? Why? She had been wound up from the scene at Theta House—but optimistic.

Now she just felt awful. Ashamed of her behavior over the past few weeks. Ashamed that Todd thought he could just snap his fingers and she'd come running.

She closed her eyes tightly and pressed her hands to them. If she could just forget. Just have a few hours of respite from the waves of humiliation that were washing over her body from head to toe.

A drink would make her feel better. At least temporarily.

But she didn't want to drink.

How was it possible to want something and *not* want it at the same time? She wanted to start over. But her old behavior patterns were so much more comfortable.

She needed to talk to somebody. Somebody who wouldn't judge her.

Alex's hand closed over the phone, and her finger punched in the hot-line number. The line rang only once before he picked it up.

"T Squared?" she said in a trembling voice. "It's Enid. Do you have a couple of minutes to talk to me?"

"For you, Enid," he answered, "I have all the time in the world."

She couldn't help smiling. "You may be sorry you said that. It's been a long day, and I've got a lot of things I need to talk about."

"Good. It's been a slow night, and I just worked my last crossword puzzle. Let me get my soda, and then we'll get started."

Alex heard him put the phone down with a clunk and then heard footsteps in the background. She felt so close to him, it was like being in the same room.

If she closed her eyes, she could picture his back as he crossed the room to get his soda. He had broad shoulders, and he wore a green knit jersey a

149

couple of sizes too large. His dark-blond hair was cut short, but the back looked a little shaggy.

More footsteps. He was walking back toward her now. She couldn't see his face because of the way the light shone, but she knew it was warm and friendly. A wide mouth. Large brown eyes with dark brows that grew across the bridge of his nose.

A face just like someone else's she knew.

"Okay," he said cheerfully. "Shoot."

She shook her head, trying to clear it. She was playing mix and match. Attaching faces and bodies to personalities, and vice versa.

"Enid?" T Square prompted. "Are you there?"

"I'm here," she answered.

"Good. Tell me everything and start at the beginning—or at least this morning."

Alex leaned back against her pillows. Maybe it was better that she didn't know what he looked like. If he really was good looking, she would be totally inhibited. It would be impossible to talk to him the way she was talking to him now. Openly. Honestly. "Well," she began, taking a deep breath, "it started this morning at my sorority house . . ."

Chapter Nine

"Kawww kawwww!"

The loud bird cry echoed through the woods, and Lila woke with a start. Her eyes blinked against the glare of the early-morning sunlight and she sat up.

The muscles in her back and arms were so sore, they ached with each breath she took. Slowly, painfully, she stretched, trying to work out some of the kinks.

It was cold. The small fire she had managed to start last night had long since gone out, and there was nothing left at the center of their little camp except ashes and lightly charred green wood— which was all she'd been able to find.

She glanced upward and groaned. There was a huge dark cloud in the distance, and it looked like it was moving their way. All they needed now was rain or snow and they'd never, ever get another fire going.

Bruce stirred slightly and groaned. Lila crawled over to where he slept in a huddled heap and gently shook his shoulder. "Bruce? Bruce? Are you awake?"

Bruce's lids lifted heavily. "Mmmmm," he grunted.

"How do you feel?"

"I don't know yet," he whispered.

"Can you get up?"

Bruce's dry lips moved slightly, but he said nothing.

Lila put her hand to his forehead. He was still hot. Still feverish. But was he worse than yesterday?

"Bruce?" she said a little louder. "Can you get up?"

"I need to sleep," he whispered. "Just let me sleep."

Lila stood up and began to pace. She had never felt so helpless in her life. What was she supposed to do? She didn't know anything about fevers or illness or anything else. She didn't know whether she should be trying to keep him warm or cool him down.

Somewhere along the line she must have been taught something about first aid. Girl Scouts?

Health class? Her mind quickly scanned her childhood files and came up blank.

She couldn't remember a thing. Nothing. Couldn't remember what to do for a puncture wound. Couldn't remember what to do for an abrasion. Couldn't remember what to do for a burn or a fracture, or a sprain. And worst of all, she didn't have the slightest idea what to do about a fever.

She was so famished, she could hardly think straight. Never, in her whole life, had she been so hungry.

Bruce needed food if he was going to get better. And Lila needed food if she was going to take care of Bruce.

She was going to have to forage for something in the woods. And who knew what was out there. Lila paced the perimeter of their camp, walking back and forth and wringing her hands in an agony of fear and indecision.

She felt her back teeth grinding. Damn him. If he hadn't tried to show off and pretend he knew how to fish, he wouldn't have fallen in the water and gotten this sick.

It was all his fault. All his fault that they had crashed. All his fault that they had no provisions. All his fault that he was going to die.

And because of his incredible stupidity, Lila was going to die too.

Every vestige of sympathy disappeared, and it was all she could do not to walk over and kick him where he lay shivering on the ground.

It was time to think about survival for real, she thought grimly. This spot was obviously not visible. The helicopter had missed them, and she hadn't seen or heard another one.

Maybe she needed to move to higher ground. It would be colder, but she might be easier to see from a plane. She cast a look at Bruce.

He was too sick to travel. And if she left him, God only knew what was liable to happen. He could die of exposure. Or the wolf might come back. But staying here to protect him pretty much guaranteed that if he died, she would die with him.

If she moved to higher ground and a helicopter spotted her, she could lead the search party back here to find Bruce. *Or what's left of him,* her mind added.

"Shut up," she said bitterly.

"I didn't say anything," Bruce mumbled.

"Bruce," she said. "I'm going to try to find help."

He turned fitfully and said something.

"What?" she snapped.

"Don't leave me," he whispered hoarsely.

"I have to," she said. His heavy upper lids

lifted and he gazed longingly at her. For some reason, it made her want to burst into tears. "I have
to go," she choked out.

The next thing she knew, she was running.
Running away from the camp. Away from Bruce.
Away from responsibility.

She ran blindly, like a panicked animal. She had
to find food. She had to find help. It was incon-
ceivable that she, Lila Fowler, was alone and without help in this horrible nightmare.

She wondered what her parents were doing
now. Were they as frantic with fear as she was? Did
they miss her? Was her father calling all his friends
in Washington, D.C., to enlist the aid of the army
and the coast guard and the forest rangers?

No. He wasn't. Because there was no reason
for him to think she was anywhere but around the
Sweet Valley University campus.

She fell forward on the ground and began to
sob. "Oh, Tisiano," she choked out. "Why did
you die and leave me? Why?" Her fists beat the
ground as she wept.

Minutes later she lay exhausted, drifting off into
a dreamlike state. Her eyelashes fluttered down,
and when they opened again, she gasped in ecstasy.

She wasn't in the woods. She was back on the
stone terrace of her villa in Italy. The villa she had
shared with Tisiano.

A warm breeze blew over her shoulders and lifted her hair. She turned and gazed out over the ocean, which sparkled like a vast blue sapphire, glinting in the sun. Several yards from the beach she saw Tisiano's broad, tanned shoulders stroking through the water as he completed his customary morning swim.

"Signora?"

Lila turned and saw Gino, Tisiano's elderly butler, rolling the breakfast cart toward the terrace.

"Breakfast!" she cried happily, pulling her silk robe tighter around her. She hurried over to the scrolled iron table and chairs, where two beautiful place settings were laid out for breakfast.

The butler held her chair for her and then handed her a large white linen napkin. With a grand flourish, he lifted the silver dish cover and revealed a huge tray of eggs and sausages. He lifted the lid of another tray, and Lila's mouth watered at the sight of a luscious fruit salad.

The butler took one of the delicate porcelain cups from the table and filled it with steaming, rich hot coffee from a silver pot.

Hurry, Lila thought as the butler rearranged the silver forks and spoons on the table and corrected the arrangement of butter plates and salad bowls. *Hurry up and serve breakfast. I'm hungry. I'm so hungry.*

But her Italian still wasn't very good. She couldn't figure out how to tell him to get a move on. All she could do was smile encouragingly and hope he understood.

But the butler continued to move at his own maddeningly stately pace. He rearranged the chairs. He rearranged the sausages on the serving platter. He rearranged the flowers in the center of the table.

Hurry, Lila thought again, almost sobbing with impatience. *Serve the food. What are you waiting for?*

The butler wiped an invisible speck of dust from Tisiano's coffee cup.

Tisiano! Of course. That's what he was waiting for. He wasn't going to serve breakfast until Tisiano joined her at the table.

"Lila!" she heard a voice behind her cry. "Wait for me. I'm coming."

Her heart lifted happily. Tisiano was through with his swim. They could eat now. She turned in her chair to watch him run toward her, with water dripping from his sleek body.

But when she turned, it wasn't Tisiano running toward her. It was Bruce. He lifted his hand and waved. "Lila! Wait. Wait for me. Wait, Lila!"

The elegant terrace receded into the distance. The butler rolled the breakfast cart away, and she began to weep with disappointment as cold wind replaced the temperate breeze.

Lila jerked awake with a start, and her fingers flew to her eyes. She didn't know if she had been dreaming or hallucinating, but her tears were real.

"Lila!" she heard again. "Lila! Wait for me."

She looked around her in confusion. Was she still dreaming? Still hallucinating?

Then her wet eyes widened in horror. Bruce was stumbling through the trees in her direction. He was so weak he could hardly walk, but he doggedly pressed on. "Lila," he was crying hoarsely. "Lila, don't leave me. Lila, wait."

Her first response was anger. Why did he have to come blundering behind her—ruining the only happy moments she'd had since the crash and probably just making himself worse?

Another sob rose in her throat, this time a sob of guilt and frustration. She had always been selfish. But not even she was selfish enough to go off and leave Bruce to take his chances with the elements and the wildlife. She had to stay with him. Even if they both died.

"Lila!" he cried again. "Please wait. I'll keep up. Don't leave me behind."

A cold, sickening dread began to steal over her

limbs. Bruce Patman looked like a dead man already.

Jessica held up a red ribbed tank top and frowned at her reflection in the mirror. "Nope," she decided, throwing the tank top in the direction of all the other rejected garments.

The door opened and Elizabeth appeared. She looked around the messy room and began to laugh. "You're in a good mood this morning."

"How can you tell?"

Elizabeth crossed to her own bed, picked up all of Jessica's clothes and accessories, and dumped them on her sister's bed. "I don't know why, but the happier you are, the messier you are."

Jessica grinned. "I am in a good mood. My history professor didn't show up for class this morning—which means I have no classes today. I'm meeting Isabella and Denise for lunch at Theta House—where I'm now a pledge in good standing. *And* I have a date tonight with James." She held up a long-sleeved white blouse and black leather vest. "It's shaping up to be what I'd call a perfect day."

Elizabeth sat at her desk and began unloading her backpack. "What are you doing with James tonight?"

"We're going to dinner at the Mountain Lodge Inn," Jessica said.

"Wow! Fancy. What's the occasion?"

"We're celebrating my victory and Alison's defeat." Jessica felt a little shiver of happy anticipation. The Mountain Lodge Inn was the most elegant and romantic—not to mention expensive—restaurant within a thirty-mile radius of Sweet Valley University. It was high up in the mountains at the end of a twisting, turning road.

A slight crease formed between her brows. That road could be tough to negotiate if a driver weren't absolutely stone-cold sober.

Except when he drinks, she heard Courtney's voice repeat again.

She felt her pleasure slipping away. Then she mentally shook herself. It was silly to worry. Courtney didn't know what she was talking about, and besides, Isabella had told her that Courtney had dated James briefly at the beginning of the semester. She was probably jealous and trying to spoil Jessica's relationship with him.

Sure, James had gotten a little drunk the night of the Zeta party. But her date with him last night had gone without a hitch. He had been a perfect gentleman. Besides that, he was a lot of fun to be with. He listened to her when she talked. He laughed at her jokes. And he looked at her as if she were the most beautiful girl he had ever seen. It was hard to believe he was the same guy who'd been acting like a loud and rambunctious jerk.

It had probably been because all his friends were around, Jessica decided. All guys were like that. It would be stupid to make a big deal out of it.

"Mmmmm." Elizabeth smacked her lips. "I wish somebody would take me to the Mountain Lodge Inn right now. I'm starving, and the food there is supposed to be great. What are you going to have?"

Jessica pulled on the white shirt and tugged at the collar. "I don't know. I called Lila, since she goes there all the time. But I guess she's still not back. I know she said she liked the salmon. On the other hand, the steaks are supposed to be the leanest and tastiest in the state."

Elizabeth rifled the top drawer of her desk. "Aha. I knew I had ten dollars stuck in here somewhere." She shut the drawer and flipped her hair off her shoulders. "Well, while you're lunching with Isabella and Denise at Theta House, I'm going to be dining on *pain au gratin* at the cafeteria."

"*Pain au gratin?*"

"A grilled cheese sandwich." Elizabeth grinned. She slung her backpack over her shoulder and stuffed the money into her pocket. "I've got a history lecture right after lunch, and unfortunately *my* history professor is punctual to a fault. Bye!"

"Bon appétit!" Jessica joked. As soon as the door closed she transferred an armload of clothes, shoes, and accessories back to Elizabeth's bed. Jeez! How did Elizabeth expect her to get dressed with all that mess in her way?

"Alison Quinn is a pain in my you know what," Denise said a half an hour later as she and Isabella and Jessica sat at the little round kitchen table in Theta House.

In front of them was a bowl of tuna mixed with lite mayo, a fruit salad with no sugar, and a box of low-fat breadsticks. Jessica wanted to save her appetite and her calories for the Mountain Lodge Inn.

"If I were you," Denise continued, "I'd give her the boot." She reached for a breadstick and broke it with loud snap.

"What about you?" Jessica asked Isabella. "What do you think I should do?"

Isabella ruffled her dark hair with her perfectly manicured fingernails. "It's a tough call. You gotta remember, you're only a freshman. You're going to be in this sorority for four years. Two years from now—scratch that; make it *six months* from now—nobody's going to remember who did what to who. Or who did what first. Or whether or not Alison deserved it—which she does. All people are going to remember is that you, Jessica Wakefield, blackballed a sorority sister."

Jessica reached for a breadstick and nibbled it thoughtfully. "Good point."

Denise leveled her own breadstick at Isabella. "You're right. But if she *doesn't* ax Alison, she's going to have to watch her back for the rest of college. Alison's not going to take her licks and then shake hands and make up. The minute Jessica lets her off the hook, Alison will be hatching some new plot to make Jess look bad."

Jessica reached for another breadstick. "That's a good point too," she murmured. She lifted the breadstick to her mouth and then lowered it. This whole thing was beginning to ruin her appetite. "What am I going to do?" she cried in frustration. "It's a lose-lose situation."

Isabella sat back in her seat and crossed her arms over her chest. "At least you know what you're dealing with."

Jessica shrugged. "So?"

"So you're getting a little bit of revenge already," she said.

Jessica smoothed the cuff of her silky white blouse. "I'm not following you."

"Me neither," Denise said.

Isabella sat forward and rested her elbows on the table. She began delicately picking the strawberries out of her fruit salad. "You know Alison better than Alison knows you—which means right now she's really sweating this. How could she possibly know what you're planning to do about her when even you don't know what you're planning to do about her?"

Denise smiled. "I get you. In other words, she's at Jessica's mercy and doesn't have any idea what to expect."

Isabella nodded. "That's right. And whatever you decide to do, this is the worst part for Alison. She's used to calling the shots and being in control." Isabella smiled. "The suspense is probably killing her," she whispered.

The three girls laughed, and Jessica felt some of her anxiety slipping away. "Let's talk about something else for a while," she begged. "Please. Alison is a barracuda, and I don't want to ruin my perfect day thinking about her."

"Is today a perfect day?" Isabella asked.

Jessica reached behind her and rapped her knuckles on the butcher block. "So far, so good. Knock on wood. And tonight is going to be a perfect night."

"What's going on tonight?" Denise looked at Isabella. "Is there something going on tonight?"

Isabella shrugged and lifted her brows at Jessica. "What happens tonight?"

"I have a date," Jessica said happily.

"With James?" Isabella asked.

Jessica nodded. "We're having dinner at the Mountain Lodge Inn."

"Oooh la-la!" Denise waved her hand, letting the thumb and forefinger waggle.

"Wow!" Isabella whistled. "That place is pricy. Sounds to me like James is pretty serious."

Jessica felt her pulse give a strange little worried bump. She hoped he wasn't feeling *too* serious. James was great. A really, really great guy. And she liked a lot of things about him. But it was too soon after Mike for her to be serious about anybody.

"Hello?" Denise said, cupping her hands like a megaphone. "Earth to Jessica. Are you in there?"

Jessica blinked and laughed. "Sorry," she said. "I was just thinking."

"About James and the Mountain Lodge Inn?"

Jessica opened her mouth to speak, but before she could answer, they heard the front door open and a laughing, chattering bunch of girls came hurrying into the kitchen.

Each girl smiled and gave Jessica a friendly greeting as they pulled up chairs to join them at the table.

"Where has everybody been for the last two hours?" Denise asked.

"There's a band on the quad," Kimberly answered. "They just finished."

"We missed it?" Denise moaned.

"I didn't know anything about it," Jessica said.

Tina Chai reached over and took a cherry off Jessica's plate. "Nobody did. This quartet just set up and started playing."

Somewhere in the house, another door opened. Jessica heard the sharp click of heels tapping along the dark wood floor of the hallway. Just outside the kitchen, the steps paused. As the door swung open, Jessica glanced up. A puffy-eyed Alison Quinn stepped silently into the room.

Alex's lungs felt like they were about to explode in her chest. Her feet felt like she had lead weights in the soles of her shoes. And her arms felt so fatigued, she didn't think she was going to be able to hold a pen when she sat down to study tonight.

She let out a loud groan as she began her fourth, and last, lap around the quad. "How did I get this out of shape?" she asked herself.

The day had gone pretty well. Two classes. Lunch. An hour in the library and then back to her room.

It was the *back to her room* part that had threatened to derail her fresh start. All that peace and quiet gave her too much time to think. And the more she thought, the worse she felt about the way she'd been behaving lately. Then she wanted a drink.

Her first impulse had been to pick up the line and call T Squared. But they had spent two hours on the phone last night, and she didn't want him to think she was totally neurotic.

Her next impulse had been to throw in the towel, fish her old pal out from under the bed, and have a good stiff drink. But she'd come far enough that she hated to blow things for herself. She knew she should throw the bottle away. But she wasn't ready to give up her security blanket yet.

The last impulse had been to dredge up her old jogging clothes and go for a good long run. She hadn't done any serious jogging in a long time—not since she started going out with Mark and turned into Alex the party animal.

"Hi, Alex!"

Alex looked up and saw Noah giving her a wave. The next thing she knew, she tripped over her own feet and fell facedown into the dirt.

Her nose squashed painfully into the hard ground, and she could feel the late-afternoon damp seeping through her running clothes.

Next to diving across the kitchen at Zeta house, this is the most embarrassing thing that's ever happened to me. He's going to think I'm a complete idiot, or else an incurable dipsomaniac.

She tried to climb to her feet. But when she put her hands down to push herself up, her arms were so weak from the unaccustomed exercise that she couldn't even push her upper torso up off the ground. She just lay there, flailing in the dirt like a sea lion beached on dry land.

"Having some trouble?"

She looked straight in front and saw the thick white soles of a pair of high-top black sneakers. *Please don't let that be Noah,* she pleaded silently. *Please!*

Two strong hands closed around her upper arms and began hoisting her to her feet.

When they were face-to-face, she smiled weakly. "Hi, Noah."

"Hi, Alex."

"I don't know what happened," she said breathlessly. "One minute I was running and the next minute I was on the ground. But I don't want to keep you from whatever you're doing. And I hope you got the Coke out of your shirt yesterday. Did you? You know, I don't fall down every day. Just every other day—ha ha." She was babbling, but she couldn't stop.

He frowned and studied her face intently while he checked for cuts or abrasions. Finally he seemed satisfied that she wasn't really hurt. He pulled a red bandanna from his back pocket and began to dab at her nose. "You're okay," he explained. "You've just got some dirt on your face."

Noah put his other hand gently on her chin to steady her face and grinned. He had a nice grin. When he smiled, his whole face smiled. His brows went up and his eyes crinkled at the corners. "It's clean," he said, nodding toward the bandanna. "I promise." He dabbed gently at her forehead. "And yes, I got all the Coke out of my shirt. No problem."

Three female joggers passed them by, and Alex watched their graceful form and great figures. Her own body had developed a few lumps and bulges over the last few weeks.

Noah replaced the bandanna and looked down, obviously trying to figure out what had tripped her. His black sneaker smoothed out the rough track, and he shot a glance at Alex.

Alex felt her face flush red. There was nothing on the ground to explain her fall. Was he thinking she'd had a drink?

"I fell over my own feet," she explained.

He didn't immediately respond, and Alex felt a rush of inexplicable fury. It was like he didn't believe her. "I did," she insisted defensively. What was the use of trying to make a fresh start and stay off the booze if people were going to just think the worst anyway?

"Hey! I know," he said kindly. He put a hand

on her shoulder. "Believe me, I've wiped out on this track myself a couple of times. The ground gets worn down and there are a lot of slick spots."

A lump rose in her throat, and she felt like crying. She liked Noah, but it seemed she was just destined to make a fool out of herself every time she was around him.

"Thanks," she said, backing away. "Thanks. I think I'm all right now."

He took a step forward and opened his mouth to say something else, but Alex didn't wait to hear. She was afraid she was going to burst out crying and look like an even bigger wacko.

"Alex!" he called after her. "Alex, wait!" But she kept running. She veered off the track and angled in the direction of her dorm. She wiped furiously at her eyes to clear away the blur of tears.

She kept running when she hit her dorm and hurried up the stairs, taking them two at a time. Several of her dormmates cast curious looks at her, but she didn't pause long enough to let anybody ask any questions.

As soon as she was in her room she slammed the door shut and threw herself facedown on the bed. "What's the matter with me?" She sobbed out loud. "It's like I'm totally losing control of my emotions and my body and my mind."

It was like the ultimate case of PMS. This was

almost as bad as the drug withdrawal she'd gone through sophomore year in high school. She remembered how depressed she'd been when she finally flushed all her pot and pills down the toilet.

An invisible hammer came down and clunked her right on the top of her head. Her breath caught in her chest, and she sat straight up. "Of course!" she said aloud. "This *is* drug withdrawal."

The sudden revelation brought her tears to an abrupt halt. Why hadn't she seen it before? People were always saying alcohol was a drug. She'd just never thought about it that way. And she never bothered to hide her drinking. She connected drugs with the idea of sneaking off and smoking pot or taking a pill in secret. When it came to alcohol, she let the whole world view her stupid self-indulgence.

She felt strangely relieved. If this was drug withdrawal, she knew from experience that it was survivable. It wasn't pleasant. And fighting the impulse to pick up the drug again was an emotional roller coaster. But she'd done it before, and she could do it again.

Understanding her feelings made them a lot easier to cope with. She had an overwhelming urge to talk to somebody who could understand what she was going through.

She picked up the phone and began to dial.

"May I speak to T Squared?" she asked breathlessly.

"I'm not sure he's here. Let me check," said an unfamiliar voice. Alex's heart hammered inside her ribs. Was he there?

She heard the sound of footsteps, a door opening, and male voices greeting each other. The footsteps came back. "He just walked in. Hang on two seconds, will you?"

"I'll hold," Alex agreed.

A few moments later someone picked up the receiver. "Hello?" He sounded breathless.

"I'm just calling to tell you I'm not neurotic," she said happily.

"Enid?"

She laughed. "How did you know?"

"Just a wild guess. How are you?"

"I'm good but not good. I figured out why the last twenty-four hours have been such a wild ride. And I don't know why I didn't see it before."

Alex sat down on the bed. "When we talk," she said, "we always start with the present. But today, if you've got the time, I'd like to start at the real beginning."

"Sure," he said in a serious tone. "We'll talk about whatever you want to talk about."

Alex paused and bit her lip. Then she plunged in. She told him about her friendship with Elizabeth. What a gift it had been in high school.

How Elizabeth had believed in her and made her feel confident. Competent. Pretty and popular.

But that friendship had been hard, too. Hard to be best friends with someone who was always more popular, more beautiful, more talented, and more respected than she was.

She also told him about her past drug experiences. And how hard it had been to stop.

And then she told him how she'd embarrassed herself that afternoon in front of the guy she'd spilled a drink on before. When he asked for details, she clammed up. "It doesn't matter exactly what happened," she said. "Believe me, I know when I wind up looking like a jerk."

"You really like this guy, huh?" T Squared asked.

"I like him a lot," Alex answered softly.

"So you've been a little clumsy or said the wrong thing. Big deal. You think this guy never did anything dumb? If you like him, tell him."

"I'd rather die," she said bluntly.

There was another long pause. "You don't trust him, do you?" His voice sounded almost sad.

"Don't trust him?" Alex repeated.

"Right. I think what you're saying is that you're afraid to open up to him because you don't trust him."

This time, the long pause was on Alex's end of

the line. "I think you're right," she said.

"Speaking from a guy's point of view, I know that really hurts. Like this one girl who always assumes I'm thinking the worst and runs off before I—"

"Before you what?" she asked. It was nice to have T Squared revealing *his* inner feelings to *her* for a change.

"Wait a second." He laughed. "We're talking about you, not me. Now why don't you give this guy you like a chance?"

Alex closed her eyes and saw Noah's face studying hers. She saw his eyes search the ground for an invisible obstacle and then turn a speculative gaze on her face. She shook her head.

"I can't hear you if you shake your head," T Squared reminded her.

"I think he's written me off," she said softly.

"I think you should talk to him before you draw any big conclusions."

"I can't," Alex choked out. "I just can't. You're right. I don't trust him. I don't trust anybody right now—except you," she added. "I trust you, T Squared. Maybe because you don't know who I am, and I don't know who you are. I can't let you down. And you can't betray me. Right?"

"Right," he answered gently.

Chapter
Ten

When Alison saw Jessica, she froze in the doorway of the kitchen and the smile abruptly left her face. All the girls in the kitchen became quiet, and there was a long silence that seemed to go on forever. Kimberly and Tina got quietly up from their chairs. "Excuse me," they both said softly, heading for the back door.

"Chickens," Denise hissed.

Nobody laughed, and Jessica wished she could sneak out the back door too. As much as she despised Alison, she didn't like being drawn into a face-to-face confrontation. And what Isabella had said made sense.

Next year there would be a lot of new girls coming into the sorority. If Jessica had a reputation for being vindictive and a blackballer, people might put her in the same category that they put Alison in now.

Alison's hard glare broke into a sickly sweet smile. "Hello, Jessica. Wow! I love your outfit. But then, you've always got on something that looks great. You have terrific taste."

Jessica wanted to retch. Alison was so incredibly transparent. Did she really think flinging Jessica a few compliments now would undo all the damage?

Maybe she did, which just showed Jessica how right Isabella and Denise had been. Alison didn't know her at all. And she had no idea what Jessica was going to do.

Jessica met Alison's eyes with a cold stare. "Knock it off, Alison."

The smile left Alison's face, and she turned pale.

"I'm glad you're here," Jessica continued, "because I've got something to say to you. Something important."

Pam Stanger stared intently in Jessica's direction and looked almost eager to watch her give Alison the ax.

Everyone else stared determinedly at the floor, obviously uncomfortable watching somebody get the boot—even if it *was* Alison Quinn.

"I've given this blackball option a lot of thought," Jessica said with a poker face.

"And . . . ?" Alison's eyelid began to twitch,

and Jessica felt Isabella's foot nudge her under the table as if to say *See, the suspense is killing her*.

No doubt about it. Isabella had been right. Nothing Jessica could do to Alison could be worse than what she was doing now.

Jessica tossed her hair off her shoulders and played with the gold chain trim on the pockets of her vest. So far, everything she had said was true. She had been giving the blackball option a lot of thought—she just hadn't reached any conclusion.

Alison nervously wet her lips. "Jessica," she began in a wheedling voice. "Sometimes sisters fight, but that doesn't mean they can't make up and be friends. Nobody should know that better than you. Look at you and Elizabeth." She forced a laugh and looked around the room for support. "Right?" she added, hoping to prompt a response.

Nobody laughed, and Jessica continued to stare icily at Alison. "For your information, Alison, Elizabeth has never set me up to commit a crime and then framed me."

There were several gasps.

"I'm not sure that after that even *sisters* could make up and be friends."

"Couldn't they *try?*" Alison pressed, practically begging now.

"No They couldn't. I don't think you and I will ever be friends . . ."

Alison's shoulders slumped and her face sagged. It was almost pathetic, Jessica reflected. "But that doesn't mean we can't keep on being sisters," she finished.

The lowered heads jerked up in surprise. "I'm not going to blackball you," she said. The relief on everyone's face was obvious, and Jessica was glad she'd decided to be magnanimous.

"But . . ." Jessica continued.

The girls froze.

"I'm not going to let you off scot-free, either. I get to pick a punishment, right?" She looked to Isabella for confirmation.

Isabella nodded. "I'm pretty sure that's what Magda would say."

"Anything," Alison said gratefully. "I'll do anything, Jessica. Your homework. Your laundry. Wash your Jeep. You name it."

Jessica leaned back and smiled, twirling a strand of her hair. "You were always so nice to me when I was working as a waitress at the coffee-house, I thought it might be nice for you to find out what it's like to stand on your feet during an eight-hour shift."

Alison groaned while the rest of the girls began to laugh and applaud. Alison was infamous for the snooty, imperious way she spoke to people she considered beneath herself—like waitresses.

"I think I'll call Artie Stigman tomorrow and see if he can use an extra waitress next Saturday night."

There was another burst of laughter. "You better be able to cope with a party of twenty or so," Denise teased Alison. "The whole house will turn out to get a load of this!"

"Yeah. And we're not big tippers, either," Pam added.

This time Jessica joined in the laughter. She hadn't forgiven Alison—not by a long shot. But she was glad the whole episode was over and done with.

Now she could concentrate on her evening with James. While the other girls chattered and teased, Jessica turned her mind to a more important issue.

What was she going to wear?

"Lila," Bruce moaned. "Don't leave me."

Bruce tossed back and forth on the hard ground. His legs kicked restlessly, and his arms shot out now and then as if he were trying to grab something. "Get away," he said suddenly, swatting an imaginary bug. "Get away." He fell back against the ground, and his head moved from side to side. "Lila," he cried softly. "Are you here?"

"I'm here," Lila answered. But she couldn't

tell whether or not he'd heard her. He was delirious now. He'd been rambling wildly and not making any sense at all for about the last two hours.

Lila squatted beside the tiny fire she had managed to start and put another twig on it. Then she went back to her work.

She had conducted another thorough search of the wreckage and found several things that were going to be useful. Best of all, more matches.

The second-best find was a knife. A big kabar knife.

Lila turned her attention to the pilot and copilot seats. She wielded the knife clumsily, but with determination. The sharp point of the kabar sliced easily through the plasticized upholstery.

Slowly, carefully, she peeled it away from the seat, trying to keep it all in one piece. She was going to need something waterproof to wrap the matches in. And if it snowed, she'd need it to construct some kind of shed.

After the upholstery was removed, she ripped and tore through the wadding and stuffing until she got to the wooden seat frames.

"Aha!" she said with satisfaction. The roof of the cabin kept her from being able to stand. But she stooped and brought her booted foot down on one of the wooden seat frames as hard as she could.

The wood broke with a splintering sound, and Lila let out a little breath of relief. The seat frames were sturdy and solid—they would burn slowly.

After dismantling the seats, she picked up a large piece of fuselage shaped like a bowl. She tapped it with her fingernail, and it made a tinny sound. Good. She could carry water in it.

She stuck the kabar into her belt, grabbed the makeshift bowl, and hurried through the woods in the fading light.

Starvation, fear, and desperation had sharpened her wits and forced her to focus. Bruce was sick. Very sick. By tomorrow morning she wouldn't be able to leave him alone at all.

If they were going to live through this, she was going to have to use parts of her brain that she hadn't known existed. Lila picked her way through the thick leaves and overgrowth and then let out a cry as her foot tangled in a root. She stumbled and fell forward.

Stickers scratched her arms and her face, and she flailed in a thick briar. "God! I hope none of this is poison ivy," Lila muttered. She struggled to her feet and examined the brambles where she had fallen.

With a cry of ecstasy, she reached out. It was a blackberry bush. Full of big plump blackberries. Hundreds of them.

The brambles caught in her hair and scratched cruelly at her hands, but she paid no attention. With frantic haste she began pulling the berries from the vines and stuffing them in her mouth. She felt prickly leaves and even the occasional bug between her teeth, but she didn't care.

No food, in her whole life, had ever tasted so delicious. She had eaten filet mignon in Paris, beef Wellington in London, sushi in Tokyo, and lobster in Maine. But nothing in her past compared to the feast she was devouring now.

When her appetite was partially sated, she began to calm down and think clearly again. If she left the rest of the berries on the bush, would they still be here tomorrow?

She couldn't tempt fate by taking a chance. Lila unbuttoned her canvas jacket and tied it around her waist like an apron. Then quickly and efficiently, she began pulling the blackberries from the vine and filling her apron.

If she crushed some, she might even be able to get a few of them down Bruce. In a matter of minutes Lila had stripped the bush. She bundled up her jacket like a sack and slung it over her shoulder as she continued on toward the water.

She heard it before she saw it. And the very sound seemed to amplify her thirst. Still, she forced herself to follow the bank until she found some smooth, gently flowing water. She didn't want to run the risk of another accident. There was nobody to pull her out if she fell in.

When she found a safe spot, she lay down on her stomach and drank thirstily. "Ahhhhh," she breathed, letting the cold water splash over her face.

She drank again, like an animal, with her face in the water. And when she opened her eyes, they bulged in surprise. Right below the surface of the water, practically staring up at her, were two fish.

Lila froze. They looked like trout—not that she'd ever seen a trout except garnished with a lemon on her plate. She turned her head and saw another trout. And another one. And *another one*.

"My God!" she whispered. "This river is full of fish."

She closed her eyes and pictured the Bolivian jungle guide. He had given them a demonstration in catching fish without a line and hook. Straining every muscle, she reconstructed the guide's face, physique, posture.

He had stood motionless in shallow water with his hands cupped. Then, when a fish swam into the range of his hands, he sprang into action, flipping the fish up out of the water and onto the bank.

Lila sat up and removed her boots. It was

getting late, and it was cold. But she didn't have any choice. She pulled off her long underwear. Shivering, she looked cautiously around.

Don't be stupid, she told herself. *If there were anybody around, you wouldn't be in this fix.*

Without wasting another second, Lila peeled off the rest of her clothes. If she tried to sleep through the night in wet clothes, she'd wake up as sick as Bruce.

She ran down the bank another few yards until she found a shallow spot where she could safely wade out.

"Brrrr!" The water was icy cold, and she felt like her legs were being skinned.

Something slithered past her leg. Lila jumped and let out a shriek. "Calm down," she immediately told herself. "That was a fish. And fish are what you came for."

Lila kept wading until the water was at about mid-thigh level. Then she bent forward, cupped her hands, and riveted her gaze on the water.

She held her breath, trying not to move even a fraction of an inch. Soon her patience was rewarded. A large fish—a granddaddy of a fish—swam languidly toward her. His body swayed back and forth, as if he were out for a leisurely swim and taking in all the sights.

Lila forced her jaw to unclench. It was important

to stay loose. To relax. To be at one with the water.

The fish swam closer. Lila's eyes stayed with him as he moved in figure eights around her thighs.

She leaned slightly forward, conscious now of nothing but the slowly swimming fish. When it was time to act, her hands penetrated the water with precision.

There was a magnificent splash when Lila brought up her hands; the fish came flying up out of the water in a fountain. As Lila watched in openmouthed wonder, it hurtled through the air and landed on the bank of the river, where it wriggled and flopped.

"Yes!" Lila cried joyously. Stark naked, she ran up the bank, grabbed the kabar knife, and with grim determination set out to clean and gut the squirming mass.

She'd never cleaned a fish in her life. There had always been hired men to do things like that for her. Guided possibly by instinct, she wrinkled her nose and proceeded with the chore.

Once the fish was cleaned, Lila washed her own hands and arms, rolled in the grass to dry herself off, and climbed back into her clothes.

She wrapped the fish in her silk camisole and slung it over her shoulders along with her sackful of berries. Under her arm she balanced a fresh bowl of water.

On the way back she took one or two wrong turns. The next thing she knew, she was standing in a clearing that looked totally unfamiliar. "Don't panic," she soothed herself. "Don't panic. You're doing great so far. Use your senses."

She closed her eyes. She had made a straight line from their camp to the river—but the sound of the rushing water was coming from her left side.

She turned ninety degrees. Now the sound of the water was behind her.

She sniffed. In the breeze there was a faint smell of wood smoke. That meant the camp was straight ahead.

Lila began walking. The light was almost gone, but here and there she began to spot familiar landmarks.

Soon she was stepping into their camp. Bruce lay curled in a ball, whimpering. She dropped her bags and hurried toward him. "Bruce. Bruce, can you hear me?"

Bruce didn't answer, but he tossed his head fitfully.

Lila dipped her fingers into the water and put a few drops on his cracked lips. He made a noise in the back of his throat that sounded like he was pleased.

Again she dripped a little water on his lips. It took a long time, but finally she was satisfied that he'd had enough water to keep him from dehydrating.

His fever seemed worse, though. She picked up his wrist and felt his pulse. She was no medical student, but it wasn't difficult to tell that it didn't feel like hers. It was erratic and weak.

Lila located two rocks and took them over to the fire. She managed to open up a little area in the center of the flames, and she placed the rocks there. She laid the fish on top of the rocks so that the surrounding heat would cook it.

While the fish was baking, she stowed the berries high up in the overhead compartment of the cockpit.

The sun was down now, and the fire burned brightly as Lila neatened up their camp. She took the plastic from the airplane seats and put it on the ground next to Bruce. Then she rolled him over like a nurse so that he was no longer lying on the damp ground. She wrapped the blanket tighter around him. It wasn't a perfect arrangement, but it would suffice for the moment.

Lila looked around, feeling more alert and focused than she could ever remember. Being this close to death made being alive seem like a separate sensation. Her sight, hearing, sense of smell, and ability to think seemed to have been enhanced by her instincts to survive.

She couldn't depend on Bruce. Or Daddy. Or the forest rangers. All she had was herself.

The smell of the fish beckoned, and Lila hurried over to the fire and peered down at her dinner. The skin had turned brown, and when she poked it with the kabar knife, the inside was white and flaky.

Carefully she lifted the fish on the end of her knife, flipping it onto the ground. Lila ate quickly and greedily, still squatting by the fire. It took less than two minutes to eat the fish, and when she was finished, she felt almost faint with relief.

A chilly breeze blew past, and Bruce began to moan. She went over, reached under the blanket, and felt his shirt and pants. They were still damp.

She let out her breath impatiently. "I can't believe I didn't check this before. Where was my brain?" Her fingers didn't hesitate as she unbuttoned the flannel shirt. It was hard getting him out of it, but she felt strong and capable, and she wrestled it off.

Next came the khakis. They were a little harder. It was tough pulling pants off a deadweight.

She took his clothes and hung them from a nearby tree. Then she lay down next to Bruce and stretched her body out along his, molding herself against him. Her body heat should do a good job of warming him.

She watched his profile in the flickering firelight. For the last several hours she had felt curiously detached from reality. Detached from herself and from him. She was turning into something new, but she wasn't sure what it was.

She could feel his body warming beside hers, and she pressed her ear down on his chest. The heartbeat was still erratic. But it was strong.

And so was hers.

Chapter Eleven

"What about this?" Jessica turned gracefully and modeled her black flowing pants and red bustier. Over her arm she carried a little black-and-red-print bolero jacket.

"How many times are you going to change?" Elizabeth asked with a chuckle. "That's the fourth outfit you've tried on."

"I think this is it," Jessica said. "Unless you think the yellow dress looks better."

Elizabeth shook her head. "No. I think what you're wearing looks perfect. Don't change it."

Jessica stood on tiptoe and felt around on the top shelf of the closet. "Where's my black patent clutch bag?" she muttered.

Elizabeth reached over toward the pile of stuff on her bed, picked up the bag, and waved it. "Does it look anything like this?"

Jessica smiled and snatched the bag from Elizabeth. "Thanks." She began unloading some of the contents of her big leather purse into the smaller bag. "What are you doing tonight?"

"Hitting the books," Elizabeth answered.

There was a knock at the door. Jessica looked guiltily around the room. She scooped up her clothes and shoes and transferred them to Elizabeth's bed, leaving her own half of the room miraculously neat and clean.

"Hey!" Elizabeth protested.

"What's the difference?" Jessica grinned. "It doesn't matter what James thinks about *you*." She took a few mincing steps toward the door in her three-inch heels. "James," she said in a melodious voice as she opened the door.

"Hi, Jess." James stepped into the room and gave Elizabeth a smile. "Hi, Elizabeth," he said. "Nice to see you."

"It's nice to see you too," Elizabeth responded with a welcoming smile. She definitely approved of James. In fact, she approved of him so much it was scary. She wondered if she was turning into her own mother. Next to Mike McAllery, James Montgomery looked like a picture-postcard boy next door. Elizabeth was glad that her sister had somebody so attractive, so steady, and so *safe* to go out with.

His eyes swept the room, and he let out a low whistle when he encountered the mountainous pile of junk that covered Elizabeth's side of the room.

She covered her mouth to stifle a laugh. Jessica was right. The mess seemed to be a shock to his system.

That fit in pretty well with what she knew about James. He was a straight-*A* student and a disciplined athlete. He probably kept his room in practically military order.

Jessica took her patent clutch and closed it with a snap. "I think that's everything." She gave Elizabeth a wide smile. "Good night, Liz."

James practically leapt across the floor in order to open the door for Jessica. "Gosh, your sister sure is messy," Elizabeth heard him say in a low tone.

"Oh, I know," Jessica said. "And it just drives me crazy."

Laughing, Elizabeth gathered an armful of Jessica's belongings from her bed and dumped it on her twin's bed.

"Maybe I'll trade in the Jeep for a crane," she muttered as she sat back down at her desk and picked up her highlighter pen.

An hour later she had twenty pages of high-lighted passages to type into her history file. She was reaching for the keypad of the computer when there was a soft knock at the door.

Tom had mentioned something about catching up on some work at the station, and they had agreed to see each other tomorrow. Elizabeth pushed the keypad away impatiently. Jessica's friends had the annoying habit of dropping by at all hours of the day and night.

But when she flung open the door, it wasn't Isabella or Denise or any of Jessica's other sorority friends. It was Maia.

"May I come in?" she asked quietly.

"Yeah, sure. Come in." Elizabeth stepped back, and Maia walked tentatively into the room, looking around. "Is Jessica here?" she asked.

"No. She's out. Have a seat."

Maia continued to stand. She looked nervous and ill at ease. "I need to talk to you a little more about . . . um . . . what we talked about in the library."

"First of all," Elizabeth said, "I want to apologize for jumping in and pushing you to do something you're not comfortable doing. I was out of line to tell you to go to counseling or the authorities. I was out of line giving you any advice at all. I don't have any training in that kind of thing, and I should have just kept my mouth shut and listened."

Maia's lips moved slightly, but she said nothing.

"I'm sorry I was a bad friend," Elizabeth said quietly.

Maia sat down on the bed next to her. "You're not a bad friend," she said unhappily. "But I am. When I said I didn't want to name the guy, I was just thinking about me." Her eyes met Elizabeth's. "I still don't want to go to counseling, and I don't want to have to name the guy and wind up in the middle of a messy trial in which I wind up looking like a tramp. But I do want to tell you who it was. Because I think you ought to know." Maia pulled her baggy sweater closer and crossed her arms over her chest.

Maia's face contorted briefly and she swallowed hard.

"Maia?" Elizabeth prompted.

Maia's eyes dropped to her feet.

"Is it someone I know?" Elizabeth asked, feeling totally bewildered. If Maia wanted her to know who it was, why was she having such a hard time getting it out?

Elizabeth quickly ran a mental review of all the guys she had dated, all the guys she hung out with, and all the guys Tom hung out with. Had it been one of them? Was that why Maia was acting so strange? "Who was it, Maia?" Elizabeth asked slowly, beginning to feel alarmed.

Tears began to trickle down Maia's cheeks.

Elizabeth stepped forward and gripped her by the shoulders. "Maia!" Elizabeth practically shouted. "Tell me. If it's something I need to know, you have to tell me."

Maia pulled away with a little cry. "It was James," she sobbed. "It was James Montgomery."

"How is everything?" the waiter asked.

James nodded his approval and swayed slightly in his seat. "Everything's great," he said in a voice that was just a little too hearty.

"May I bring you anything else?"

James held up his empty beer bottle. "I'll have another one of these. Jessica? How 'bout you?"

How many times do I have to tell him I don't drink? Jessica thought irritably. She forced herself to smile. "I'll just stick with water, thanks."

James leaned forward and his hand squeezed her knee under the table. "Have a drink," he urged in a stage whisper. Jessica felt her face flushing furiously and could hardly bring herself to meet the waiter's eye. James was getting drunk. She'd lost count of the number of beers he'd ordered.

It was one thing to get a little tipsy at a fraternity party—but getting drunk in a restaurant seemed utterly gross.

At first, it had made her feel incredibly sophisticated to be sitting with a guy who nonchalantly ordered a drink. In fact, the whole evening had made her feel incredibly sophisticated. As soon as they had arrived, the maître d' had snapped to attention, leading them with great ceremony to their booth by the window.

Below them was the canyon, and she could see the faraway twinkling lights of Sweet Valley. Several admiring eyes had followed her unhurried progress through the elegant restaurant. She had seen lots of familiar faces, at whom she smiled blandly in the manner of Lila Fowler. It was a smile that intimated she had been to the Mountain Lodge Inn dozens of times—and while it was all very nice, she didn't consider it any big deal.

Inside, though, she could hardly contain her delight. It was the most romantic restaurant she had ever seen.

The first course had been wonderful. But by the time their entrées were served, Jessica had a strange sense that the evening was slipping out of control.

"Bring her one, too," James instructed the waiter.

"I don't want one," Jessica insisted.

But neither James nor the waiter seemed to hear.

James turned his head and gazed out the window. "Beautiful, isn't it?" He turned his attention back to her and stared into her eyes. "Almost as beautiful as you, but not quite."

It was a nice compliment—and he sounded sober. Jessica felt a little of her resentment fade.

The waiter reappeared and put two beers on the table just as Helen Peterson and Grant Walker came walking toward their table. Helen was a Theta and a senior. She'd always been nice to Jessica, but she wasn't the type to go out of her way to befriend a freshman.

Jessica reached out and firmly gripped the beer bottle in one hand and her glass in the other. "Hello, Helen," she said in her deepest and most mature voice.

"Jessica!" Helen replied in an enthused tone. She and Grant paused beside the table, and Jessica could tell by the unprecedented warmth in Helen's voice that she was taking it all in—Jessica's outfit, her date, the beer.

"Do you know James Montgomery?" Jessica asked as she tried to pour the beer casually into her glass without producing a huge head of foam.

Helen gave James a wide smile, and James immediately rose to his feet and took her outstretched hand. "How do you do?"

"Jessica, James, this is Grant Walker," Helen said.

Grant shook hands with both Jessica and James. He didn't speak but nodded awkwardly at them. Jessica couldn't help feeling pleased that James was more poised than Helen's date.

For the next few minutes James kept up a stream of easy, cordial small talk. Both Helen and Grant looked like they were thoroughly charmed.

Every trace of slur had disappeared from his speech, and he seemed alert and outgoing.

I was making a mountain out of a molehill, Jessica thought. *James is practically a grown man. He knows how much alcohol he can handle.*

Jessica made a pretense of sipping her beer while Helen and James conversed. She even took a small taste or two. It wasn't very good, and she was grateful to be able to put it down when Helen's conversation with James came to an end.

"Bye," Helen said, fluttering her fingers at Jessica. "See you soon."

Jessica fluttered her own fingers. "Bye," she echoed. She smiled inwardly. *I have the feeling Helen is going to be a lot friendlier from now on.* That was good. Even though Jessica had come out of the last battle with Alison a winner, Denise was right. It wouldn't be long before Alison began plotting against her again. Having

198

some influential seniors on her side wouldn't hurt Jessica a bit.

No doubt about it, James Montgomery was turning out to be a real asset.

Elizabeth's heart had resumed its beating. But it wasn't her normal heartbeat. It was a slow, sickening thud. Heavy dread began coursing through her veins as Maia continued her story. Elizabeth was next to her on the edge of the bed, slightly in shock.

"We'd gone to the Mountain Lodge Inn for dinner," Maia said in a choking voice. "On the way home, he pulled over. On one of the mountain roads."

Maia lifted a tissue to her nose, fighting tears. "You can get liquor there with a fake ID. James had a lot to drink. I had a couple of drinks too. I wasn't drunk, but I was . . . I don't know . . . relaxed. Being silly. I guess he took it the wrong way, and anyhow . . ." She swallowed hard. "On the way home, he pulled off the road and—" She broke off, but she didn't need to say anything else. Elizabeth knew what had happened.

"I still don't understand," Elizabeth said quietly. "Why didn't you tell?"

"Because everybody had seen me at the Mountain Inn Lodge with him. We'd been kissing in our booth. I was wearing a backless dress. Elizabeth! Nobody would believe me. They'd say I asked for it—or led him on—or even that he had dumped me and I was trying to get even with him."

It's a hell of a way to get even with a guy, Tom had said.

A sudden surge of anger and fear set her heart racing and galvanized her feet. She sprang up, clenching and unclenching her hands while she tried desperately to plan. "You're right," she said to Maia in a quaking voice. "The horrible part of all this is that I can't argue with you and tell you that you're wrong. Because you're absolutely right." *But it's not going to happen to my sister,* she mentally vowed.

Elizabeth leaned over and briskly hugged Maia's shoulders. "Maia. I'm so sorry to leave you like this. But I've got to go." She stood and grabbed her jacket off the back of her desk chair.

"Where are you going?" Maia asked as Elizabeth snatched the Jeep keys off her desk.

"To the Mountain Lodge Inn," Elizabeth answered.

"Dessert, gorgeous?"

"I'd better not," Jessica said, poking out her lower lip in a slight pout. She patted her slim waist. "I don't want to pork up."

200

James scooted out of his seat, came around, and slid into her side of the booth next to her. "Your body is absolutely perfect," he said in a coaxing voice. His hand reached behind her and caressed the small of her back. "But if you're worried about calories, I'll help you out by eating half of what you order."

Jessica laughed. James was great. But she wished he would quit fondling her in front of all these people. His hand traveled to the bare skin that showed between the waistband of her slacks and the bottom of her bustier top. Should she say something?

He lifted his other hand to signal the waiter. "Could we get a dessert menu, please?"

"Janna! Have you seen Tom?"

Elizabeth stood in the doorway of the campus television station, panting. On her way to the parking lot she'd suddenly realized that she didn't know the mountain roads very well. But Tom did.

Janna sat at a long worktable, sorting piles of scripts and notes that needed filing. "I saw him a couple of hours ago," she said. "But he just came in, grabbed some books, and then left."

"Did he say anything about coming back here?" Elizabeth asked.

"Nope," Janna muttered in a distracted tone.

She licked her thumb and then began riffling through her papers.

"Did he say anything *at all* about where he was going?"

There was a long pause, and it seemed to take Janna forever to ponder the question. "Nope," she said finally. "I don't remember what he said."

Elizabeth let out an impatient gasp. Janna was a good office clerk, but she never had any idea what was going on around her.

"Okay, listen—" she began. But she broke off when Janna showed no sign of having heard. She just continued thumbing through her pages.

Elizabeth closed the distance between the door and Janna's desk in three strides. She grabbed the papers from Janna's hand and leaned down to face her until they were nose to nose. "This is *important*. So listen to me very carefully," she said. "If Tom comes by or calls, tell him I'm looking for him and it's urgent. With me so far?"

Janna nodded.

"Good. I'm going from here to the library to look for Tom. After that, I'm going to try to find the Mountain Lodge Inn. Tell him I'll be traveling up route six. I know there's a shorter way to get there, but I don't know the roads—which is why I'm looking for Tom. Did you get all that?"

Janna blinked in confusion. "Yeah. I think so.

But wouldn't you rather write it down?"

Elizabeth was already on her way out the door. "I don't have time," she called over her shoulder.

William stepped back into the shadows and watched Elizabeth as she came running out of the station and began trotting diagonally across the quad toward the library.

Something was wrong. Something was definitely wrong. He'd watched her for so long, he felt he could read every movement of her lithe and beautifully proportioned body.

When she was in a hurry, her torso tilted slightly forward and her slim legs took long strides.

If she was tense or worried, her shoulders hunched up around her ears.

When she was frightened, her lips curved inward and her skin turned white around her mouth.

Even in the dim light of the streetlamps that illuminated the quad, he could see that her face was pale. Her shoulders were hunched, too. And as she jogged toward the library, her body was slightly inclined.

Obviously she was looking for Tom. But William knew she wouldn't find him. He had seen Tom and his roommate, Danny Wyatt, climb into Danny's car, happily arguing over whether or not

Danny could order anchovies on their pizza.

Tom Watts was a fool to go off and leave her on campus alone. Particularly when she was frightened. It would be so tempting for someone else to protect her, and in the process steal her away.

Someone with enough taste to see the perfection in her face.

Someone with a strong enough ego to cope with her incredible intelligence. Someone with enough strength of purpose to rise above the petty prohibitions that bound the rest of humanity.

Someone like him.

He broke into a run himself. If he cut directly across and went in the side door of the library, he could be inside the lobby in time to watch her come racing in.

The double-glass front doors of the library opened automatically with an electronic whooshing sound and Elizabeth trotted into the lobby, panting and grateful for the overly air-conditioned temperature.

She was sweating now—more from nerves than from heat. Every minute counted, and she felt like precious time was slipping away. Dinner would only keep Jessica and James at the Mountain Lodge Inn for so long and then . . .

Elizabeth pushed her fears to the back of her mind. If she panicked now, she wasn't going to be any help to Jessica.

A quick look around the deserted lobby told her that Tom wasn't there. Out of the corner of her eye, she caught a glimpse of a wheelchair as it slid behind the magazine rack.

Up and down she went, checking the rows of study tables for a familiar dark head and a set of broad shoulders hunched over a book.

No Tom.

I'll check the basement. Elizabeth ran toward the fire stairs and jumped down them two at a time. She pushed open the stairwell door that led to the interior of the basement reading room.

She toured the stacks and the carrels at a run but saw no one except the guy in the wheelchair searching through the periodical file.

A quick look at her watch made her heart jump into her throat. It was getting late. She was going to have to get going. With or without Tom.

As she ran back up the stairs, she wondered how that guy in the wheelchair had managed to get downstairs so quickly.

Once upstairs she hurried over to the desk where Jack was taking in returned books. He gave her a big smile when he saw her. "Want a key to a carrel?" he asked.

Elizabeth shook her head. "Nope. I'd like a map of the area, if you have one."

Jack nodded and reached under the desk. "What are you looking for?"

"I want to see which roads will take me to route six."

"Going to the Mountain Lodge Inn?"

Elizabeth nodded. "I'm supposed to meet someone."

Jack pulled out an old dog-eared map and spread it on the counter. "You going by yourself?"

Elizabeth nodded. "Unless you see Tom Watts. If you do, tell him that's where I've gone and ask him to meet me, will you? It's about Jessica."

"Actually, I don't know Tom Watts. What does he look like?"

"Tall. Very dark. Handsome. Used to be an athlete."

"I'll keep an eye out," Jack agreed. Then he put his finger on the map and began to trace. "If you don't want to fool with the traffic, you can try route twenty-seven. You pick it up behind downtown. It'll take longer, but you'll still hook up with route six."

Elizabeth nodded, studying the map. "Want to take this with you?" Jack asked.

Elizabeth hesitated a minute. "No," she said

finally. "If Tom does come by, he might need it." She nodded her thanks and lifted her hand in a gesture of farewell as she turned toward the door.

Where are you, Tom? If I've ever needed you, I need you now.

"I'm Tom Watts," a deep voice said at the desk. "Did anybody leave a message for me?"

William jumped in surprise. He had been just about to spring from his chair and run to the parking lot through the basement tunnels when the tall, slender guy who had been sitting in the magazine section sauntered over to the counter and introduced himself as Tom Watts.

The guy behind the desk gave him a big smile. "Yeah, Tom. Elizabeth wanted me to give you this map and ask you to meet her up at the Mountain Lodge Inn. Something about Jessica, she said. Need any help?"

The guy shook his head and gave Jack a genial nod. "No, thanks. I'll just take the map."

"Bring it back tomorrow if you can," Jack asked.

"No problem."

William stared as the long-legged figure strode to the library door and stepped out into the night. William pondered the mystery for a moment. He wasn't sure who exactly that guy was.

But one thing he did know for sure—it wasn't Tom Watts.

Jessica watched James warily as he tilted the brandy glass and drained it. "Ahhhh," he breathed. He slapped the glass down on the table. "Ready?" he asked.

"Ready," she chirped, trying hard to make her voice sound pleasant. She was really irritated now. She had been ready to leave for the last half hour. They had finished their dessert long ago, and then James had insisted that they have brandies, in spite of the fact that Jessica had made it clear she didn't want one.

Of course, he hadn't listened. So not only had Jessica had to sit here and listen to him drone on and on about some boring football game while he finished *his* brandy, she had to sit there and listen to him drone on and on about some boring football game while he finished *her* brandy.

And the whole time, his hands had been busy.

Jessica had said nothing, but it was going to be a relief to finally get away from his liquor breath and his hands. She reached for her jacket and waited patiently while he pulled himself out of the booth so she could stand.

He stood, stepped aside, and fell heavily to the floor.

"James!" Jessica cried. She bent over to help him up.

"Dammit," he swore. "Why the hell did they put a step there? I could have broken my damn neck."

Jessica recoiled. James Montgomery's beautiful manners had disappeared altogether.

"Here," she said quietly, taking his arm. "Let me help you up."

"I don't need any help," he said shortly.

By now two waiters were hovering. "Are you all right, sir?" the older one asked.

James stood and tried to pull himself together. He smoothed his hair and tucked his shirt down tighter into his belt. "I'm fine. I just tripped. That's all." He gave them a cold stare, as if daring them to contradict him.

Neither waiter did.

James gave them a curt nod and then took Jessica's elbow and propelled her toward the door. Once outside, he handed the parking valet the ticket for the car.

As soon as the valet was out of earshot, Jessica turned to James and gave him a million-dollar smile. "It's been such a long day for you. Wouldn't you rather have me drive?"

He cocked his head to the side and looked at her like she was crazy.

"You must be sleepy, too, after all that . . ."

His face darkened. "All that *what?*"

"Food," Jessica finished lamely.

"If you're worried about whether or not I can drive," James said, "you can stop worrying. I never drink more than I can handle."

Jessica chewed her lower lip. Two minutes ago he had fallen over his own feet. Of course, there *had* been a little platform step there. He might have tripped over that.

Watching the car come up the drive, Jessica clenched and unclenched her hands. The mountain roads were curvy and poorly lit. Could James drive them safely?

"I'd really be happier if I drove," she blurted as the car came to a stop.

James didn't answer. He handed the valet a dollar and opened the passenger side, politely waiting for her to climb in.

Jessica sighed. Short of wrestling the keys out of his hands, there was nothing she could do.

Elizabeth! her mind screamed. Of course. She could call her sister. Elizabeth would come get her.

"Wait!" she cried, putting her hand on the door.

"What now?"

Jessica nervously wet her lips. "I'd, uh . . . I need to go to the ladies' room."

210

James sighed, but Jessica didn't give him time to say anything. She brushed past him and ran back into the restaurant, making a beeline for the rest room. There was a pay phone just outside the ladies' room door, and Jessica fished a quarter out of her change purse and shoved it in the coin slot. As soon as she heard the dial tone, she frantically began punching in her phone number.

Please be home, she prayed. *Please!*

By the fourth ring, her heart dropped in disappointment. Elizabeth wasn't home. Jessica briefly debated calling a taxi, even though she knew she didn't have enough money with her to cover the cost of the ride back to campus.

She could always explain the situation to the manager of the restaurant. He would certainly make arrangements to see that she got home safely.

But if she did that, James would be furious. And it wouldn't take two days for a story like that to get around campus. James's friends would think she was hysterical and dorky, and the Thetas would be angry with her again for making a Greek look bad.

Jessica replaced the phone and trudged back out into the restaurant. It was late, and there were very few diners left.

The manager smiled and gave her a curious

look. "Is everything all right?" he asked. Jessica said nothing. She pushed open the door and walked out into the parking lot.

James was combing his hair in the mirror when she approached the car. He was so engrossed in the task, she had to tap on the window to get his attention.

He leaned across the seat and opened her door from the inside. "Welcome back," he purred.

Jessica didn't answer. She just gave him a tight smile and shut the door behind her. While he started the engine, her hands reached automatically for the seat belt. When it clicked into place, she cinched it tightly over her flat stomach.

Please don't let me need this, she prayed as the car started forward, the wheels crunching over the gravel drive.

Chapter
Twelve

"Move!" Elizabeth shouted in frustration. But of course, the driver of the creeping car in front of her couldn't hear her voice. And neither could the Jeeps on either side of her. Both cars were full of kids. Several vehicles on the road had speakers mounted on the outside, and nine different kinds of music blasted out into the night.

Someone behind her honked. Elizabeth looked in her rearview mirror and saw some jerk driving a convertible and wearing sunglasses. "Where exactly do you expect me to go?" she muttered at the rearview mirror.

Her fingers drummed rhythmically on the steering wheel. "Come on, come on," she said when the light changed and the car ahead of her didn't move.

After what seemed like ten minutes, traffic began to crawl. Elizabeth wanted to scream with impatience. She couldn't believe how much traffic there was. Everybody and his dog was out cruising tonight. The main drags of the sleepy little college town were clogged.

The car on her left turned up the volume of its radio. Elizabeth could hardly hear herself think. Just when her jangled nerves were about to snap, the lane on her right opened up.

She didn't hesitate two seconds; she jerked the wheel and pounded the gas pedal. The red Jeep lurched into the right lane.

A blue compact came zooming up and had to slam on the brakes to avoid hitting her. "Idiot!" the driver yelled.

Elizabeth ignored him and searched anxiously for another hole in the traffic. When she found it, she careened across two lanes until she hit the shoulder of the road.

Keeping a sharp eye out for the police, she executed a U-turn and began speeding up the shoulder of the road against the oncoming traffic.

When she reached the narrow alley between Oak and Third streets, she skillfully guided the Jeep past the garbage cans that lined the alley until she found herself on a dark road that ran along the back of downtown. She stepped on the pedal, turned again, and soon was hurtling up a narrow and unfamiliar mountain road.

*   *   *

William ground his teeth in anger as he watched the taillights of the Jeep disappearing in his rearview mirror. How did his goddess expect him to protect her if she was going to take up stunt driving as a hobby?

He leaned over and stuck his hand out the passenger window of the light-green Oldsmobile he had borrowed from Andrea. The oncoming traffic in the right lane obligingly slowed to let him in.

He waved his thanks and then repeated the maneuver until he reached the shoulder. Then, just like Elizabeth, he did a U-turn and took off behind her.

He wished he knew exactly what the problem was. Something about Jessica. Probably something about Jessica and that boor, James Montgomery. How like Jessica to entangle herself with such a plebeian type. A football player, no less.

In William's opinion, football players were an unfortunate fixture of college life. But women of taste and refinement seldom dated them.

Elizabeth's taste was usually faultless. Tom Watts represented a temporary lapse. Soon she would see him for the lesser creature that he really was. And she would break up with him—just like she had broken up with the other one.

She had shown excellent judgment when she

had dumped that hometown loser, Tad. Or was it Todd?

He smiled. He was convinced it was no coincidence that she had broken up with that basketball player not long after she had met himself.

Once exposed to William's charm, intellect, and discriminating tastes, it must have been impossible for her to regard that loser with anything less than utter contempt.

Up ahead, he saw her turn into an alley.

"What a chore!" he complained. All this cloak-and-dagger business was a nuisance. Still, he cut his lights so he could follow her without being seen.

A few minutes later he was climbing the mountain road behind her, hanging back several car lengths so she wouldn't catch sight of her shadow.

There was something heavy and ominous in the air, and William shivered happily like a hunting dog in the morning damp. Something was going to happen. Something was going to happen tonight to bring him and Elizabeth closer together.

All these days of watching her and following her every move were paying off. Somehow, he was going to render her a service. Some favor for which she would be enormously grateful.

Then she would forgive him for the unfortunate misunderstanding that had sprung up between them—and be his forever.

"Watch it!" Jessica cautioned.

James jerked the wheel, and the little red car skidded back into the right lane. "Sorry," he muttered.

Jessica's hands were balled into tight fists. From the minute they left the parking lot, it had been apparent that James was in no shape to drive.

Twice Jessica had actually had to reach out and pull the wheel. His right arm was draped over her shoulder and she wiggled, trying to push it off. "Try putting both hands on the wheel," she snapped. "Then maybe we could stay in our own lane."

But James just chuckled, and his big hand closed over her shoulder and squeezed.

I am never leaving the campus with this guy again, Jessica vowed. She didn't care how many dinners he invited her to at the Mountain Lodge Inn—it wasn't worth it. This whole evening was turning into a nightmare. "Please pull over and let me drive," she said, being careful to keep calm. "And you don't need to worry about the gears. I know how to handle a stick shift," she added.

James turned his face toward her and winked. "Great outfit," he said, completely ignoring what she had just said. His eyes traveled down her body. "I like a girl to dress sexy. If she's interested in sex, I think it's great that a woman feels she can make that statement."

Statement? What statement? If James Montgomery thought her clothes were stating a sexual interest in him, he was going to be a very disappointed man. Right now, she didn't even like being in the same car with him.

The car drifted into the wrong lane again. Another car was heading straight at them. "Watch it!" she cried.

A blue station wagon whizzed by, missing their car by inches. Startled, James removed his arm from Jessica's shoulders. The close call seemed to sober him slightly, and for the next few minutes he remained intent on his driving.

But when they reached a fork in the road, James bypassed the turn that would have taken them straight down the mountain and into town. "Where are we going?" Jessica demanded.

"To Lookout Point," he answered.

"I don't want to go to Lookout Point," she said bluntly, no longer caring what he thought. "I want to go home."

"Aw, come on, Jessie," he coaxed. "It only

takes ten minutes to get there, and the view is incredible."

"I don't care about the view," Jessica said stubbornly. "I want to go home."

"I'll take you home," he promised. "*After* we stop at Lookout Point."

Jessica sighed. Stopping at Lookout Point was going to mean necking. Oh, well, she'd kiss him once and be out of there. If that's what it took to make him take her home, then the sooner they got it over with, the better.

Elizabeth shifted into third and hit the gas. The Jeep was having a hard time on this steep stretch, but Elizabeth couldn't baby it. Not tonight. Every second counted.

She raced past a sign that pointed toward Lookout Point, and within a few feet she saw what she had been looking for. A wooden, arrow shaped sign that said MOUNTAIN LODGE INN: FIVE MILES.

At least she knew now she was on the right road. She let out a sigh of relief and sent up a silent prayer that Jessica and James were still at the restaurant.

James moved his mouth over Jessica's, and she did her best not to gag. "Ohhh, Jessica," he sighed as he buried his hands in her hair.

Jessica sat stiffly in her seat. She just couldn't bring herself to return his kiss. James, however, showed no sign at all that he noticed her lack of enthusiasm. He continued to cover her face and neck with kisses.

I don't know what's worse, Jessica thought, fighting tears. *Weaving down that mountain with a drunk driver or sitting here getting mauled.*

Her fingers twitched convulsively. And when his lips moved down her throat, she reflexively grabbed the door handle and pulled.

"What's the matter?" he asked.

"I need some air," she answered shortly. She gave him a slight push and then slid out of the seat. The ride had been so nerve-wracking and frightening that her legs were shaking.

She walked a few feet away from the car and looked down. Far in the distance she saw the campus lights. *Oh, Liz,* she thought miserably. *Where were you when I needed you?*

"They left? How long ago?"

The valet shrugged. "Hard to say."

"You're sure it was them?"

"Sorry, what?"

"The girl. Did she look like me?"

The valet smiled. "Yes," he said in heavily accented English. "The girl, she looked just like you. She is with a big boy—he look like a football player. They leave here in a red car."

"Do you know which road they took?"

The valet gave her a bewildered stare.

"Which road?" Elizabeth repeated in a louder voice, doing exactly what she hated when other people did it—shouting at people who didn't speak English as if they were deaf or something. She made an effort to modulate her voice and pointed straight down. "That way?" she asked. Then she pointed up. "Or that way?"

"Ahhh," he breathed. He pointed down. "That way."

Elizabeth smiled and nodded, then she revved the engine. If they were headed down, at least she didn't have to find her way through a maze of sightseeing trails along the top of the mountain.

As the Jeep pulled out of the parking lot and onto the road, Elizabeth thought she saw a large shadow in her rearview mirror. She reached up and adjusted the mirror so she had a better view. Was something back there?

The road curved around, and she almost missed it. "Oops!" she muttered. She'd better stop worrying about imaginary shadows and pay attention to her driving. A bead of perspiration dripped down her temple. She lifted her arm and wiped her forehead with her sleeve, then rolled down the window to let in the cool mountain air.

"Getting enough air?" James asked gently. He came up behind her and circled her waist with his arms. "Why don't we get back in the car?" he whispered into her hair. "It's cold outside."

"I think I'd rather stay out here," Jessica said.

He turned her around to face him and smiled. "Whatever you say, baby. If it doesn't bother you, it doesn't bother me." His hands slid around her back and reached for the hooks of her bustier top.

She instinctively pulled away. "Stop that," she said.

He laughed lightly and then tightened his arms around her, pulling her to the ground.

Jessica let out a little cry of alarm as he pushed her over on her back and rolled on top of her. His hands pulled at the waistband of her pants.

What did he think he was doing? "James!" she cried. "Stop it. Get off me!"

But James's only response was to cover her mouth with his and plant a wet, sloppy kiss on her lips. She jerked her head away and tried to sit up. "Get off me," she repeated.

She was beginning to feel scared now, and she heard a note of rising hysteria in her voice that made her even more panicky.

He had managed to unzip her pants and was trying to pull them down when Jessica began to fight; she beat on his back with her fists. "Get off me!" she screamed. "Stop!"

"Do you have any idea at all what that dinner cost?" he grunted while his hands began fumbling at the front of his own khakis.

"Stop it, James!" she shrieked.

"Hold still," he ordered. "What's the matter with you?"

"I don't want you to touch me!"

"Just because I missed a few curves in the road? Lighten up."

Jessica couldn't believe it. Couldn't believe this was really happening.

"You jerk!" she shrieked as he yanked at her underwear.

Suddenly he rolled off and scrambled to his feet. He leaned down and grabbed her by the upper arm. "It's too cold out here," he said in a thick voice. "Let's get in the car."

Jessica tried to pull her arm away, but it was no use. His hand was like a vise, and he hoisted her to her feet as if she were a rag doll.

James nearly let go when Jessica suddenly let

her weight drop to the ground. "What the . . ." Jessica half-lay on the ground, her feet dragging along the dirt. "Cut it out, Jessica!" he yelled. "Quit playing games." And with that, he simply lifted her up and carried her toward the car.

"No!" Jessica shrieked as loudly as she possibly could. "Leave me alone!"

Elizabeth slammed on the brakes and listened hard. Was that a scream? It sounded like a woman's scream. But then again, it could have been a bird or an owl. She held her breath, straining her ears.

The air was still and quiet. It was like the night was holding its breath in fear too.

A second scream pierced the night, setting off a flurry of bird cries. Elizabeth's heart leapt up into her throat. No doubt about it, that was a scream. And it sounded like Jessica.

Where had it come from? Which direction?

There were more cries now, and they seemed to be coming from the left.

Trying hard not to panic, Elizabeth began careening down the mountain road. Within a few yards her headlights illuminated a fork in the road where a sign pointed the way to Lookout Point.

If a guy wanted to park, that was the place to

do it. Elizabeth turned the wheel and accelerated again.

The red Mazda was parked a few yards away from the railing. Elizabeth brought the Jeep to a halt and reached into the glove compartment for the toolbox. There was a pretty good-sized wrench in it. Now that she had found Jessica, her hysteria had begun to subside a little. She was surprised that her hands didn't shake or falter.

Neither did her legs when she jumped to the ground and ran to James's car. One look inside told her everything she needed to know. She tried the door. It was locked. "I hope you've got insurance," she muttered as she lifted the wrench.

"No!" Jessica shouted. "Get away from me!" James's hands were everywhere. She felt like she was about to vomit.

All of a sudden the window on the passenger side shattered with a splintering crash. Safety glass flew in every direction and peppered them both.

Jessica screamed, and James let out a grunt. In front of Jessica's astonished eyes, his body flew back and banged against the door.

The next thing she knew, she saw Elizabeth's face through the window. Both of her hands had a grip on James's tie. Immediately she turned it like a screw, tightening the tie until she had him in an efficient choke hold. He let out a drunken protest, and his hands pawed clumsily at his neck, trying to break Elizabeth's grasp.

"Elizabeth!" Jessica sobbed.

"Come on, Jess. Let's go home."

With trembling hands Jessica fumbled with her clothes, pulling up her bustier and fastening her pants. She grabbed the door handle and climbed out, casting a last wary look behind her.

James was struggling hard now, pulling at his collar in an effort to loosen Elizabeth's hold. "Let go of me, you . . ."

"Get in the Jeep," Elizabeth instructed through gritted teeth. She was straining every muscle to keep her grip on James.

Jessica hesitated. Elizabeth had him now, but what was going to happen when she let him go? "He's drunk, Liz," Jessica warned. "There's no telling what he's liable to do. When you let go, run as fast as you can."

Elizabeth nodded. "Start the Jeep," she managed to say, her arms shaking with the effort of keeping James's huge body pinned against the door.

Jessica ran to the Jeep, jumped into the driver's seat, and started the vehicle. "Come on!" she shouted. "Let's get out of here."

*   *   *

Elizabeth opened her hands and released James's tie. She turned and ran as fast as she could toward the Jeep. Ahead of her she saw Jessica slide across the front seat to the passenger side.

Behind her she heard the door open. James came barreling out of the car like an enraged bull out of the chute. She could hear him running behind her. His feet were amazingly light for such a big guy. With a sinking heart she remembered what had made him such a valuable player. His size and his *speed*.

"Hurry!" Jessica shrieked.

Elizabeth felt a hand reach out and take a swipe at her head, missing her by inches. Then . . . there was a *thunk*, followed by a gasp of pain.

Elizabeth felt the ground shake as James landed on his back.

She couldn't help casting a look over her shoulder. It looked like he had gone down backward. Maybe he'd hit his head on a low-hanging tree limb.

But there aren't any trees in this little area, Elizabeth thought as she jumped into the car and threw it into gear. The tires spun in the loose dirt a few times before the treads dug in and propelled the vehicle forward with a jerk that made both twins' heads snap.

Elizabeth turned the wheel, making a wide circle, and almost hit the brakes when she saw what looked like a tall male figure standing back in the shadows. "Jess!" she cried. "Do you see . . ."

But Jessica didn't seem to be listening. She grabbed the wheel and turned it toward the road. "Let's *go*," she urged.

Seconds later the Jeep zipped down the twisting mountain road. Beside Elizabeth, Jessica wept softly. But Elizabeth was too busy navigating the roads to console her. Right now her first priority was getting safely back to campus before James recovered his wits and decided a car chase was the only way to repair his dented machismo.

"Lila," Bruce cried. "Lila. Are you there?"

"I'm here," Lila answered softly. "I'm here, Bruce." His head moved fitfully, and his feverish body began to shudder again.

"Lila! Lila! We're going to crash. Cover your face! We're going to crash!" His arms and legs began to thrash in delirium. "Cover your face!" he sobbed.

"We're not going to crash," she answered. Her voice broke and she paused, swallowing hard to keep from bursting into tears herself. "We're on the ground," she soothed. "We're on the ground, and we're safe."

At least for now, she added silently. Lila wrapped her arms more tightly around him and pressed her body against his under the blanket. This must be the longest night of her life. *Please let us both live long enough to see the morning,* she thought before closing her eyes to sleep.

Chapter
Thirteen

"Jessica," Elizabeth soothed. "It wasn't your fault."

"Yes, it was," Jessica sobbed.

The minute the girls had arrived back at their dorm, Jessica had jumped in the shower and stayed in there until the hot water gave out. Then she dried herself with a fluffy towel, pulled on a fresh, long-sleeved flannel nightgown, and insisted that Elizabeth help her change her bed so that she could sleep on clean sheets.

"I should have known," Jessica choked out as she tucked the sheets on her side of the bed into the mattress.

"Jessica! You couldn't have known. It wasn't your fault. You didn't do anything wrong." Elizabeth tucked in the sheets on her own side and then came around and hugged Jessica. "It's okay now," she reminded her. "You're home. You're safe. You don't ever have to go out with James Montgomery again."

Jessica's face crumpled. "How could I not have seen it?" she wailed. "You'd think that after Mike, I would have some kind of sixth sense about men. Be able to spot the troublemakers." She sniffed and dabbed at her nose with a tissue. "If it hadn't been for you, Liz, he might have . . . he might have . . ." Jessica broke off, unable to finish.

"Not just might have," Elizabeth answered bluntly. "Would have. He would have raped you."

Jessica gasped. "How do you know?"

Maia's worried face flashed in Elizabeth's mind. Maia hadn't wanted anybody to know what James had done to her. She'd only told Elizabeth in order to save Jessica from suffering the same vile act. Was it really Elizabeth's right to tell Jessica now?

Studying Jessica's desolate face, Elizabeth made a decision. She wouldn't tell Jessica now. She'd at least wait until her sister could be calm and rational. And she'd make sure it was okay with Maia first.

"The same way I knew to come looking for you tonight," Elizabeth answered. "I have psychic powers when it comes to matters having to do with my twin sister."

"You were incredibly brave," Jessica said thickly. "You're the best sister in the world. I can't believe you came after me all by yourself."

Elizabeth frowned. "I can't either," she said slowly. "In fact, I can't get over the feeling that there was somebody else on that mountain to-night. Did you notice anybody there when you stopped to park?"

Jessica shook her head and climbed underneath the covers of her bed. "Not a soul."

A sudden soft knock at the door surprised them both.

Jessica gasped and held up her blanket protectively.

"Relax," Elizabeth said, heading for the door. "Nobody can hurt you now. Okay?"

Jessica smiled thinly, but nodded. "Okay," she said quietly.

Elizabeth cracked the door and frowned. There was no one in the hall. She opened the door a little wider and something fell against her foot. When she looked down, she recognized Jessica's little patent leather evening bag. "Jess!" she whispered. "Did you leave your purse up there on the mountain?"

Jessica pulled the blanket up under her chin. "No. Now that I think about it, I left it on top of the telephone outside the rest rooms at the Mountain Lodge Inn."

Elizabeth lifted her eyes and met Jessica's. "Well, somebody brought it back."

Jessica hopped out of bed and padded toward Elizabeth. She took the purse and popped the little gold clasp. "Oh, my gosh. Look!" She reached in and pulled out several ten-dollar bills clipped together. A piece of paper under the clip read SWEET VALLEY TAXI SERVICE, 556-9874.

Jessica's bewildered eyes met Elizabeth's. "What does it mean?" she wondered.

Elizabeth shook her head in confusion. "Someone is telling you next time don't take a risk, take a cab instead."

"Who?"

Elizabeth opened the door a little wider and looked down the hall. It was empty. "Whoever was on that mountain tonight with you, me, and James."

How will Jessica handle what happened at Lookout Point? Find out if James gets what he deserves in Sweet Valley University #11, TAKE BACK THE NIGHT.

SIGN UP FOR THE SWEET VALLEY HIGH® FAN CLUB!

Hey, girls! Get all the gossip on Sweet Valley High's® most popular teenagers when you join our fantastic Fan Club! As a member, you'll get all of this really cool stuff:

- Membership Card with your own personal Fan Club ID number
- A Sweet Valley High® Secret Treasure Box
- Sweet Valley High® Stationery
- Official Fan Club Pencil (for secret note writing!)
- Three Bookmarks
- A "Members Only" Door Hanger
- Two Skeins of J. & P. Coats® Embroidery Floss with flower barrette instruction leaflet
- Two editions of *The Oracle* newsletter
- Plus exclusive Sweet Valley High® product offers, special savings, contests, and much more!

Be the first to find out what Jessica & Elizabeth Wakefield are up to by joining the Sweet Valley High® Fan Club for the one-year membership fee of only $6.25 each for U.S. residents, $8.25 for Canadian residents (U.S. currency). Includes shipping & handling.

Send a check or money order (do not send cash) made payable to "Sweet Valley High® Fan Club" along with this form to:

SWEET VALLEY HIGH® FAN CLUB, BOX 3919-B, SCHAUMBURG, IL 60168-3919

NAME_____
(Please print clearly)

ADDRESS_____

CITY_____ STATE _____ ZIP_____
(Required)

AGE_____ BIRTHDAY_____ /_____ /_____

Offer good while supplies last. Allow 6-8 weeks after check clearance for delivery. Addresses without ZIP codes cannot be honored. Offer good in USA & Canada only. Void where prohibited by law.
©1993 by Francine Pascal   LCI-1383-123